PICTURE THIS

Written by:

Jamel Rogers

Chapter 1-

INTENSE DREAM

The land was just as wide and blue as the sky. The sky was grassy and green as the land. The peculiar switch of the two left me anxious the more that dream fast forward. I walked with wings planted on my back while walking on a cloudy pathway. All of this had to mean something and I mean the message I have been waiting for. I considered myself a dream enthusiast and a guy that loves to report on the very thing against reality. Dreams. My name is Jim and I found this dream so very imaginable that it became my reality.

Why can't I feel my natural body and flesh? I felt lighter than a kite against the wind. My inner thoughts were written right in front of me and instantaneously poof into thin air like magic.

Suddenly, the dream went away and all I saw was a blacked out picture. With sweat drenching me like a pool, my eyes blinked open.

I immediately gazed into my dream journal. While looking out my bedroom window, I noticed the sun changing the color of its ray of sunlight. Oddly, that same ray of sunlight occurred in my dream a few weeks ago. I shrugged my shoulders and went on to start my morning off for school.

Then, the words inside my journal flew at me like a herd of pigeons. I noticed outside of my window everyone having a device in the palm of their hands and I was the only kid in my grade level with decent handwriting. I begin to write.

The front page of my dream journal writes:

A world like today solved by the great scheme of world wars and politics. A world without devices and technological efforts. Those people took pride in their work enough to redo a draft or solve a problem.

I was in my room feeling dreary from my tired finger tips. I bended my finger back and allowed it to soothe before moving onto the next page in my journal.

"Now, where was I?" I asked myself.

<u>NAME: JIM / DATE: 4/03/3000 / DREAM JOURNAL</u>

I began walking on a cloud of marshmallows. The marshmallows were falling down as if sucked by a vacuum. Scared as I would be, I quickly jumped from one clouded marshmallow to the next. I remained the age of 15 and began to watched these faces stared down at me laughing and laughing. It reminded me when I got up to present my project and kept sweating nervously as my peers laughed. What could this all mean? Or just maybe, it doesn't mean a thing. Just maybe. I am still not certain.

By the way, let me tell you this, I would rather pinch myself until I started feeling reality kicking in instead of these mixed messages lately.

"Time for school, son!" My mom yelled.

"I want to go to an actual school and not in some lame spaceship." I argued.

"Well, I wish I could home school you son. I do have a meeting to run to. My holographic coworkers do have a mind of their own, you know." My mom said laughing.

"Ooh that sounds nice. Can I come?" I asked.

WOOSH! The spaceship hovered over my room. I climbed out from my bedroom window after getting dressed for class.

"Guess, that's a no! Time to learn about the last time we all seen normal around here. Too bad, we are nowhere near that advance to make a time machine." I said to my mom before boarding the ship.

Once I boarded the ship, my best friend Mel gave me a high five with his invisible gloves as a practical joke. My hand raised up and swung against his hand as no contact was made. It was more shocking than our houses and surrounding buildings hovering at a thousand feet from mother earth.

"Impressive, Mel. You sure got gadgets up your sleeve. All of that is way too advance for me." I said.

"You got that right. Meanwhile, our president is made of metal with a few screws missing; if you ask me." He said laughing.

"No need to sugar code it. He's already a robot." I said as we continued laughing.

"Come on kids. Time to wear your suits. There's a lot of radioactivity around this ship. You all know the rules. It's practically imbedded in your brains." Our teacher Mrs. Mathews said towards us.

I walked in between the dividers in front of me. I slipped into my suit that felt like a bright white suit an astronaut would wear. It was very tight like slipping your hand underneath a sofa as if you're looking for loose change. By the way, the only change we have today is virtual coins. I heard a lesson about bitcoin the other week and even that seemed a bit normal unlike nowadays.

"So, you are always mentioning normal this and that. I feel like us being born in the late twenty nine hundreds bro is our way of normal." Mel said.

"Do you understand where I'm coming from?" Mel soon asked.

"Not quite. Not at all. My lost friend." I said.

"I am not lost, bro. I'm just trying to prevent a nervous breakdown from happening... Again." He said after a long pause.

"That was only bad gas in front of everyone. The teacher even got everyone thinking it's a leak from one of those monitors controlling the ship." I argued to Mel.

"Yeah right." Mel said.

Once everyone had their space suits guarded tight on themselves, we were ready for class. The ship proceeds to lift all the way above the clouds. Looking outside my side window, I see clouds similar to my dream. I was too afraid to have every single classmate think I'm psycho and a mindless complainer. It just seems like everyone is content the way the world is running on motor oil and gas leaks. That is what we get for over indulging into technology. It is just like the old saying went; one man trash is another man treasure. The big pro and con taunting us without even a bit of concern. My mind complained as our teacher showed us how to properly code flying food which seemed a bit concerning.

"Ewe. Why this garbage?" I asked aloud.

Shortly, I covered my mouth.

I was so disappointed at my disruption.

"Care to share us a more reasonable lesson, Jim?" Our teacher Mrs. Mathews asked after my snarky remark.

"Nope. Sorry, it won't happen again. Don't need you to laser beam me out of my seat for the fifteenth time." I said as I laughed.

Everyone looked at me with a straight face and the quietness of the room shortened my odd laugh.

"Okay. Well, you may continue Mrs. Mathews. Flying foods should be coded before they go extinct." I said jokingly.

"Are you feeling well?" Mrs. Mathews asked.

"Yes. I am. I just want to get on with the lesson." I said.

"Okay if you wish. Then, let's continue." Mrs. Mathews said eyeing me scornfully.

I leaned over in my holographic chair to my left to whisper toward Mel.

"What's up with the staring?" I asked him.

"Quiet. I can tell she has her ear sensors on that can hear up to a ten miles radius." He warned me.

"I have no idea what any of that has to do with the staring. Can no one take criticism?" I asked.

"Criticism should be spoken in the eyes of one another. It should never be said behind their back, Jim." Mrs. Mathews said.

She had showed off the new food gadget to us. It's called Voiceful Chewing Gum. To my understanding, you chew and it either project or slowly silence your voice as you speak. I smirk as I was just as impressed as the rest of my classmates.

It was clear as day she heard our conversation.

"Can I ask you an important question? I don't want to alarm you." I asked Mrs. Mathews.

"Yes, anyone is free to ask as much as their heart desires." Mrs. Mathews said.

"Okay, is it safe to chew gum that's also been man made in some kind of lab?" I asked.

"I mean, that seem a bit bizarre to try in front of us." I added with my eyebrow raised.

"Jim, you are dismissed once we land over to your address. I'll have to have a holographic talk with your parents, young man." Mrs. Mathews said as her eyebrows did the exact opposite.

Mel looked over at me shaking his head. I stared back in disbelief.

"Wow. Just wow." I said.

My teacher saw there was an emergency in the right corner of the spaceship and tapped her watch as she teleported in a blink of an eye. As her body once vanished, a large amount of debris fell at her exact spot.

My eyes rolled and I stepped out of the digitalized classroom full of holographic calculators along with desks and chairs.

Mel insist I stay in there with the rest of my peers.

As I wave in front of the sensors for the bolted door to pry open, Mrs. Mathews teleported back in front of me with her hands on her hips.

"I'm in trouble. Am I?" I asked.

"You bet." She said.

I stared down in sadness and twisted anger.

"No way. No way." Mrs. Mathews said repeatedly.

My eyes squinted and my face twisted up.

"What do you mean no way?" I asked.

"I tapped into our digital bookshelves and notice a book titled: The Plague That Started It All. It seems like a great read. An ancestor of mine published it in two thousand and twenty." She explained.

"You're just messing with me, aren't you? I didn't hear about an audio book since I was two years old. I get it. I'm in trouble and need a consequence. Ooh, maybe take all my gadgets while you're at it." I insisted.

"I would if you were my child. I'm your teacher so you may have to talk that up with your parents." She said.

"Good Luck! They have virtual holographic meetings twenty-four-seven these days." I replied while my arms folded.

"I know you're a good kid at heart. You are just angry with the world, but I'll let you weigh in on a little secret." Mrs. Mathews said.

"What's the secret?" I asked.

"Technology was made to bring people together and not tear us apart. Everyone, you all have witnessed a complete misunderstanding to Jim's rage against technology." Mrs. Mathews said.

"Stop using me as a life lesson that keeps making mistake after mistake! I'm not your lab experiment!" I shouted.

"Oh really? Is that what you think I see you as?" Mrs. Mathews asked.

"I know you think that of me. You think we're all just a bunch of meaningless robots created to make the world safe and easy lived. You are wrong to keep us in this bubble of delusion." I ranted.

Mrs. Mathews laughs up a storm as I hit my fist against the wall in front of me.

Mel is looking at us as his mouth was watery and drip saliva all over the floor in complete shock. We were like fire and ice or electricity and a puddle of water. We were just meant to cause outburst.

Our principal was a bit odd even for us to still handle. This was an extra-terrestrial they found on earth years ago.

“Enough humans. Enough.” The green alien said as the doors flew open.

Our faces stood stern as it repeated its words.

“Enough. Enough.” It said.

I know you all must be shocked. I am as well. I still can’t believe they trust a spaceship school of humans to an alien as a principal. Like I said, I wish things went back to whenever normal was still a thing. The insane part is there hasn’t been sight of any other alien but this particular one. Therefore, we gave that particular alien the title of either Principal Aileen or Dr. Aileen.

“Can I just go home now?” I asked Principal Aileen.

“Yes, you may. Specimen Jim.” Principal Aileen told me.

The alien smiled standing only three-foot-tall and eyes looking a bit like two sticks sprouting out of its face. Its mouth sat on the entire dome we call a head.

The ship hovered back over to my house. I hopped through my bedroom window and pretended to be sleep the rest of the day before my parents got the report from my teacher. I looked up at my televised ceiling. The big figures of my parents entered the screen above me through a facetime approach.

“Had a good day at school, Jim? Care to share us what happened?” My mom asked with her arms crossed.

“No ma’am.” I said.

"Hey, you know how I feel about smart mouths. You answer me mister." My mom said.

"End Call, Siri." I said

My voice command completely turned off my televised ceiling. I laid there letting the weight of stress toward everyone fly off my shoulders.

I clap my hands as mist surrounded the room. I close my eyes dreaming I was on an island somewhere on a foggy day. My room became decorated digitally just like the dream. The walls seem invisible that if I walked toward it I would hit my head. Luckily, I haven't lost all my marbles to get to that point in my life.

As I laid in my warm comfy digitalized bed, I sat and imagined what life looked like before all of this. I thought about everything that could've lived here. My dream snuck in some old visuals of dinosaurs, cavemen, and even gorillas. They all must've came and hung out around each other during the early two thousands. Just maybe that life died out for this life to exist today in the year three thousand.

"That's nice, just the relaxation I needed." I said to myself as I smiled.

Moments later, a loud extensive siren disrupts my happy moment. I was beyond irritable and shortly put on my silence headphones to get back to my daily nap.

Unfortunately, my parents zapped me right into their high-tech sky mobile shipyard. They warned me there was an imposter amongst us that isn't from this time.

"Yeah, this is definitely a big hoax. You selling your digital collection again, dad?" I asked.

"Don't sell yourself short, your parent already the best in the business." Dad said.

"Does that mean I could quit school?' I asked.

"No, you can't kiddo. You think we're going to waste the family genes on a dropout and not a scholar with the techno device crew. However, you kids refer to it now." He said while I gave a crooked smile.

"It's just that, I think I'm more than just a tech-whiz and instead an actual writer. I am lost in this world everyone calls home. Nothing seems to satisfy me like it used to." I said toward my dad.

"Well son, that may mean you are growing up fast. This means something like technology was better before you could walk, son." My dad said.

"Really?" I asked.

We sat in the sky mobile shipyard. The bubble stood high up and spread across the same size as a football field.

"Son, your father was trying to say that maybe you are looking at this too negative. That's all. If anything, you're more connected with everyone because the invention of electricity and gadgets." My mom said.

"Okay but I still think we are all brainwashed until proven wrong." I argued.

"No sir, nobody is wrong in this world. We have the internet for that." My mom replied.

“When is this imposter thing over?” I asked huffing and puffing.

“Right about… Now.” Mom said soon as we were zapped back into our home above ground.

Chapter 2-

BRAIN STORM

"Why the long face?" Mel asked me.

I dropped my head as I slowly snapped my finger. Mel and I stood in my room pod; a room that is highly controlled by technology.

The screen light shine so bright at Mel from behind me it was like I was standing in front of the gates of heaven.

A typed screen appeared behind me wrote out:

"Happy Birthday Jim! Way to stay strong in everything you do! From Mom and Dad." The screen voiced in the tone of my parents.

"It's the weekend and your birthday! Wow, how come I never known this? We should be having fun. Feeling mopey is not the plan at all." Mel replied.

"No, it's not that I don't like my birthday. I feel guilty of always nagging about the life I have this year in three thousand." I said.

"Well you shouldn't. Everyone has freedom of speech somewhere. We can ask your parents while we're at it." Mel said.

"Too late for that. Chances are, they are out to another planet like Saturn. They are probably trying to figure out a gadget to bring air, water, and vapor over to that planet." I said.

"Yeah, you know you too smart to be feeling mopey about a generation created by smart people." Mel said.

"You think anyone creating these ticking bombs were smart? I want you to know that they were just some lazy bums." I explained.

"Lazy, but smart at the same time. Still counts, Jim." He said.

Suddenly, we stopped in our footsteps as a quake in the sky rattled my bedroom.

"Sky quake! Hurry, we have to zap up to outer space for certain. I don't care if I vaporize." Mel said with no care.

Splat! Clack! A huge pink gummy like object hit my bedroom window before shortly slithering down in its own liquidation.

"Yuck." I said as my stomach turned.

I saw each pink beanbag hitting the window this time in packs of three. I ease up to the window sill and another fired at me behind my window. I backed up and notice that enormous brains were falling from the sky.

"I don't know Jim. I'm freaking out. No sight of our parents around and I'm freaking out. We have to call somebody!" Mel exclaimed.

Soon enough, the sounds of crackling ice hit the top of my house and frequently jab the sides of my home. It was getting worse and worse and both of Mel and I kept feeling queasy by the sight. This might be the end all that I was afraid of experiencing sooner or later.

"Mel, I'm scared." I said.

"You scared? Nonsense, I'm fine." He said as his hands were shaking and neck twitching.

"Well I am. Wait a minute, can brains cause that much damage?" I asked Mel.

"Some may cause damage depending how hard you hit your noggin." Mel said laughing.

My face scorned at him while my eyes was looking straight through the temple of his skull.

"Okay I get it, bad timing." Mel said scratching his head.

"Thank you." I said.

"You think we should try going to lower ground and I mean beneath the ground. These brains could suffocate us against our will." Mel suggested.

"Glad to see you taking this so well. Try that noise cancelation helmet I have on the shelf there. It may keep your mind at ease, bro." I said.

"Nice, I'll try it." Mel said reaching for the helmet.

Two holograms beamed from the very center of my room. It was my parents looking scared to death. They let out a huge scream as the hologram vanished before I could let out a sound.

"Okay, now. It's the time to freak out." I said falling to my knees weeping.

I was sobbing and clenched my head as my hands laid firmly around my head.

"Alrighty, we are too ahead of ourselves. Honestly, I think the brain storm is over. Our madness must've quiet it minutes ago. I never been so thankful to be human than this moment." Mel said to cheer me up.

"Yeah, I can finally ask out Myra. I had a crush on her since we entered Mrs. Mathew's class." I said looking out my window smiling.

See, each year as we proceed to another grade level we enter our own spaceship and the size depends on both height and width. It's a very crucial process we all had to participate since the year two thousand and five hundred.

"You think we should look it up? What causes brain storms anyhow?" I asked.

"I have no clue. I think this might have been practice or some sort of simulation in case a real storm happens." Mel explained.

"I'm glad somebody is looking at it better than I thought they would." I said smirkingly.

"Okay wise guy. How are we going to go jet pack flying now? Don't you want to take flight for your sixteenth birthday?" He asked.

"Yes and no. I don't think we should leave yet. My parents may be back soon. They probably sent that hologram to scare us." I said.

"You sure? Your parents aren't that devious." Mel said.

"It's all fun and games though. They're going to give us some moon pies and gather around with their birthday jingle. You watch." I said while Mel folded his arms.

We waited watching the center of the room. After five short minutes passed by, Mel went to grab a soda from a push of a button. It was delivered to him as it sat in a incubator inside my bedroom wall.

"I'm getting a bit tired. You want to jet fly instead? And if they show up, we will come back in a safe landing on the platform." Mel said.

"Sure. Do we have enough jet fluid?" I asked.

"Because, I don't want to get an injury while I'm out there." I explained.

"Yes, my dad refills mine and I got an extra somewhere in my garage." Mel said.

"Do he have more for that extra jet pack?" I asked once more.

"Yes he does. Although, we may have to fly in your side of town. He's in an important meeting. His room is full of flat screens and computer servers." Mel warned.

"Yeah that's no problem. Let's head out." I said.

I hope Mel didn't think it was my first time jet flying. Kids at my school go nuts about their first time since the age of ten. I just never trust one to give it a chance. The economy been very down lately since it's easier as ever to steal computer money. That's why I dislike a system full of wires and coding. Everyone around think it's the best thing on the block or otherwise call it a diamond in the rough. It's sad I'm the only one with my eyes woke and others bow down to it everyday like some kind of peasant to their royal king.

We took the Sky Raiser which was a machine that acted like those ancient elevators back in the eighteen fifties. The Sky Raiser has a speed of nearly a thousand miles per hour through the sky. Mel's house was pretty far, but with this machine we would get there in about a minute or two. The fun part is that it seems fast looking in through the outside than how it operates in the inside. We were like the two thousandth participant to get on this contraption. The Sky Raiser only went up or forward depending on the map it takes us through. The inventors passed away not too long ago.

After stalling for about ten minutes while we were standing by Mel's entrance, I decided to take off without warning. I beamed out the door and my speed caught up to me almost running into a skylight in the middle of the plane intersection. We were up a couple of feet from our houses having the time of our lives. I kept looking forward while Mel smiled looking down from the clouds.

"That doesn't worry you at all?" I asked him.

"No sir, I'm flying higher than a shooting star. Yippee!" He screamed.

I laughed settling down in one spot as I put the jet pack in neutral. This particular spot sat in the mist of clouds surrounding me like a whirlpool of condensation.

Something very odd seem to hover us and as the object fell I began to worry. I dodge it as much as I could and caught a glimpse of another big pink brain falling overhead. It must've been an aftershock from the last time

Mel and I was stuck in the brain storm. We hurried back with our jet packs and luckily nothing was coming down whatsoever.

As we got closer to my home platform and coming for a straight landing, a brain shortly rained down it's slimy and clear liquid. We landed and opened my front door as my parents faces were much of concern in the middle of their birthday jingle for me.

"What happened you guys?" My dad asked us.

"Ran into a new brain storm. What are they doing now? Are they creating storms by the minute?" I asked both my parents.

"No sir, our job don't determine the weather. I do see some smart kids raining down with their dumb behavior. Why didn't you guys waited until we teleported back here?" My mom asked us calling Mel's parents.

"Is that brain liquid safe from the experiment, anyhow?" My dad asked whispering in my mother's ear.

"Quiet down, you're going to scare them." My mom whispered back.

"We can hear you two." Mel said.

"Yes, sorry sweetie. Your parents will be here soon. Apparently, your mom got caught up with a lot of digital assignments at her job." My mom told Mel.

"You two will be just fine. The perfect thing is you both found yourselves back here safe and sound." My dad said.

His armpits were now two wet spots as big as his arms sleeve.

"How about we meet back after you two get washed up?" My mom asked.

"That's fine." I said.

"Cheer up though kiddo, we're definitely going to celebrate your special day!" My mom exclaimed.

Mel took my parents Switch-A-Wash which was another invention created by an urban child in the late two thousand six hundreds. It started as a toy and nowadays became an important machine to our society. Switch-A-Wash is a multi water head system that allows you to stand on two giant foot holders. This machine spins you around while each water head clean every bit of your body. We have three of them in my house. I stood on one across my bedroom. It got the job done in a jiffy.

I got dressed in my favorite fit which was a loose sweatsuit that felt nice and cozy. This suit had its own heating and cooling system inside the comfortable fabric. It was very new upon the twenty nine hundreds. Mel borrowed some of my dad stuff since he was a bigger size in clothing. We met back up at the dinner pod. My dad had the moon pies just as I expected and they all sung for me their own birthday song.

"Thank you all! I got my best pal here and two parents that finally came through!" I exclaimed.

"You're welcome son. You sure getting older now. Finally becoming a man, I see." My dad told me.

"A man indeed." I said.

My dad smiled tearing up and hugged me. My mom sat back and watching as tears ran down her cheeks as well.

"Now, I know this generation of techno gadgets isn't as fun as you thought it would be. As you get more along, you may actually start to see yourself enjoying the three thousands even more. Just watch." My mom said not forgetting about our last talk.

Soon enough, Mel's parents showed up. They were not pleased that we took the jet packs without permission. They did however greeted me with a birthday greeting and told me that they give us a pass since it was a special day.

I noticed something a bit strange in everybody's eyes as a green foggy substance surrounded their pupil. I blinked again and again to see if I was imagining it. It now weighed in as my mood silence the entire room. Everyone suddenly muted their conversations toward me and I became aware about the dangerous game technology is playing on us. The irony from my mom saying all this cool stuff about it and now I may have came across proof of just how much we use it and the damage it's causing us.

"Son you're alright?" My mom asked.

"I'm fine. I may just need a night sleep." I said.

"Hey Jim, if you need company, Mel is free tomorrow if he and you wanted to have a sleepover or just hangout whatever you boys do nowadays." Mel's mother, Sarah, chimed in.

"That is so sweet! I'll love to have Mel stay with us." My mom said nodding her head.

Mel's parents took the Sky Raiser back to their place. I got out the blankets for the extra air mattress in my bedroom. Mel got ready for bed and almost tripped himself in the hallway with the moving floor frame. Fortunately, he caught himself staying at least half wake.

"Mel, is everything good out there?" I asked toward the hallway.

"Yeah, I'm just a bit out of it." He said.

"Okay, wanna watch a film tonight? I asked.

"I got a lot of programs on my televised ceiling." I added.

Two best buds went from stuck in a brain storm, jet pack flying, and now a rocking sleepover. We somehow stayed up due to the winds rattling the house. The insane noise was like a kid shaking a box of presents on Christmas Eve. We talked about the girls we were going to talk to next time we showed up in Mrs. Mathew's home shuttle. Instead of saying home room, we say home shuttle since it's on a spaceship and there is shuttles surrounding it.

"You know, sometimes tight space suits doesn't always need to be a bad thing. I mean, it's a space suit and that is how awesome it gets out here." Mel told me.

We laughed and suddenly quiet down trying not to wake up my parents.

"You think you have all the gadgets. Check this out!" I exclaimed.

I waved my hands in the form of a wave.

A blue tight ocean wave from my inside walls appeared realistically as the motion poured toward the center of the room. It was getting a bit too realistic for Mel that he almost started freaking out.

I closed my fist having the wristband remote control around the palm of my hand.

“Relax, it’s just special effects.” I said.

“Yeah bro. I’m frightened, but it is a neat trick to add to the room.” He said.

Chapter 3-

A RACE THROUGH TIME

A game we played in gym class. It was called A Race Through Time and it was something I felt like a professional at. We got into four lines and ran through dividers that could slow you down from the race if lasers targets you. I loved every minute of it. My strategy was to try to pace myself and dodge every laser beam.

"Nice job, Jim!" Mr. Blank shouted to me at the finish line.

"Thank you, sir." I said.

"You're welcome kid. You are quite the sprinter. This was a fun experiment to see whether or not some of you would slow down or pick up speed." Mr. Blank said to me and the rest of the class.

Shortly after, we was dismissed from gym and back into home shuttle for lunch. We got back into our space suits since we do gym in a space at the bottom part of the ship. I put on my space suit and notice it was a size bigger than last time. I began to think maybe this whole time it was more my weight than the suit.

"Hey Mel, do I look different to you brother? I know it's odd to ask but I notice something about my suit." I asked him.

No response was given. Mel eyes were wide awake and now his veins turned a dark cue of blue before heading back onto the ship. I had a strange feeling he was in complete shock and maybe expose to something deadly. I called over our teacher Mr. Blank and he ran for a nearby first aid kit. We got him bandaged up and he slowly start coming back to his original self. I was fully relieved that I caught it just in time for recovery.

"Well, that almost scared me half to death!" I exclaimed.

"Yeah, no kidding. I'm glad somebody was concerned unlike my peers." He replied.

"You know us kids. We all self absorb and have such a short attention span. We were a lost cause from the start." I said jokingly.

"You do realize you're talking about yourself too as well, right?" He asked.

"Yes sir." I said bursting out laughing.

Mr. Blank gave me his card before heading back to the home shuttle.

Apparently, each space shuttle have a competition with one another playing A Race Through Time. This may be the only thing I participated in school ever.

On the other hand, I notice the girl in the decorated space suit. Myra was a very pretty girl that kept herself well kept with makeup and had a pink space suit. I went up to talk to her during our lunch break. I didn't know why I waited until now to talk to her. All these gadgets they make now and they can't come up with a confidence booster to be invented.

"Hey Myra, how are you enjoying your lunch?" I asked.

"It's gross. It taste like plastic!" She exclaimed.

"Well, I can grab us another plate. I mean, grab you another plate." I replied.

She smiled through the space helmet as her cheeks were red.

"I'm fine. Thank you though for looking out!"

"You're welcome."

"You that guy that made the disruption the other week. You seem very smart and you were great out there during the race in gym." She said fulfilled with compliments.

"Maybe we can hang out sometime. Take a ride through the old Sky Raiser if you may." I said.

"I will have to take your word for it and see. Sounds like a lot of fun!" She said.

Her friends giggled. One friend named Liz tries to move the group elsewhere. Myra stayed in that exact spot and tried to kiss me through the space helmet.

Liz and the rest of their friends sat behind us.

"Ooh I see a love connection." Liz said.

Liz smiled over at us while Mel was busy trying to keep his bandage unnoticeable.

"Girl, a lab team couldn't create that." Another friend named Jenna chimed.

Lunch was over, but being the mischievous kid I was expected to raise suspicion.

"Wanna Skadattle?" I asked.

"Yes, please!" She exclaimed.

We snuck out the shuttle before Mrs. Mathews returned from the corner of the ship. The corner of the ship is where teachers meet up to talk or do digital assessments.

We snuck to the only place we couldn't be exposed as easily. This was the bottom of the ship. Myra and I made out in the dead center of the gym shuttle. A camera weighed in on us and our images spread around the entire oval like ship. We were zapped in our respected homes and dismissed for the rest of the day. Our teacher gave us a stern lecture through a hologram in both our bedrooms at once.

I apologized on my end, so I'm assuming Myra did the same for Mrs. Mathews.

"It won't happen again, Jim. Will it?" Mrs. Mathews hologram asked.

"It won't. I just get these feelings that I can't control sometimes."

"Well, welcome to being a human. See you back in my home shuttle in five days and try to stay out of trouble." Mrs. Mathews said before her hologram vanquished.

How did this happened? I thought I'd never get caught in a time like this. I trace back through my memory and it hit me just like that. The cameras must've spotted Myra and I. That was the key thing that got me in trouble. I can add that to the bucket list of reasons I don't trust techno gadgets. Everybody hee-hawing about techno this and gadget that until they technically get mind controlled by everything around them. Sorry for the rant, but I had to get that off my chest.

A new me entered my mind and I made it certain from this point on I will play everyone's yes man game. I will be vulnerable by technology and let it control my actions since it's the only thing people could admire. I stood proud and tall as I left on the Sky Raiser toward Myra house. I figure I call her on the way there to see if she wanted to hang out. I thought her and I can kill some time now we're suspended from school.

I checked my wrist phone and seen I got fifteen missed calls from Mel. This gadget was actually a birthday gift from both my parents. You can tap a number of somebody else with a wrist phone and poof a small hologram of them shows up hovering your wrist. It's the coolest gift I ever received lately.

"What's up with the missed calls? Is your wrist phone broken?" Holographic Mel asked.

"Yeah I'm sorry man. I was kicked out of school temporarily and couldn't talk to anyone as of this point." I said knowing deep down I was lying to myself.

"Yeah right, you mentioned that girl Myra a lot. I hope she don't get you in big trouble." He said.

"Yeah. Well, gotta blast." I said after ending the call and his hologram vanished.

Wow, that was a close one. I thought to myself who to call next and my short term memory had kicked in when I realize to call Myra to see if she can hangout.

I tapped the number and a small hologram of Myra appeared in tears.

"What's wrong, Myra?" I asked.

"I'm fine. Really, I just want to hang out with you if you're still free today. I can't stay in this toxic household. My parents barely notice me with all their techno gizmo stuff around here." Myra said weeping.

"Yes, totally understand. I'll be over there in a hurry." I said taking a step out my door and out onto the Sky Raiser.

I put in the address and the tube took me all over the sky and even around a flock of birds as well. I forgot it was migrating season soon anyhow.

I ringed their doorbell and she comes to the door without a tear in sight.

"Wow, you sure cheer up quick."

"Anytime I get a chance to go outside. It's sure better than being locked in Professor Gadgets Laboratory." She said making a funny pun.

"I totally understand, my parents are now starting to notice the more and more I get in trouble." I said.

"Yeah on the bright side, it brought us together." Myra said winking at me.

"It did, but the other bright side is we don't have to go through it alone."

Without another word, she ran into my arms and hugged me tight. I rubbed her back for comfort and we decided to jet pack. I forgot to give Mel back those jet packs earlier, but I'm sure he won't have a problem with me borrowing it and easily returning it where I found it.

I had no clue why Mel was suspicious of her behavior lately. I thought things went perfectly natural with our slow attraction for one another.

"Jim, can I ask you something?" She asked.

"Sure." I said.

"You know how I was frustrated earlier through the wrist phone?" She asked.

"What's the matter? Everything alright?" I asked worried.

"I'm just going to say it. Mr. Blank is my dad. Him and I had an argument over you. Protective dad stuff you know."

"Awe man, I hope this doesn't affect my spot in the Race Through Time competition coming up soon. I been practicing my sprinting lately." I said waiting for her to laugh.

She did the exact opposite and nearly scratch my face off. I kept backing up and backing up from those long polished finger nails.

"You worry about a stupid spot and not the girl you might lose because she have such a protective dad."

"I love both those things. Wait a minute, when you became my girl?" I asked her.

"Really?"

"Yes. Just promise me this though. Your dad won't hunt me down, will he?"

“No he is not a murderer. He just want to meet you sometime but he can be a little manipulative. Just watch out for any weird things.” Myra warned me.

“What can be weirder than our lives now? Flying houses, jet packs, Principal Aileen, and more. This as weird it can get if you ask me.” I said as she giggled.

“Well you haven’t met pops yet, because that man got some secrets of his own.” She said.

“Wait you starting to scare me. What type of secret do he have?” I asked.

“You didn’t hear this from me, but he’s in love with robots and I mean in love with them. He divorced my mom for a robot and it totally broke her heart.” Myra said.

“Oh no, that is strange. Well, good thing you not like him right?” I asked.

She gave me a crossed eye look and I began to scratch my head.

“Yeah, I admit what I said was a bitty bit unnecessary. Sorry!” I exclaimed.

“You lucky, you cute. Don’t make references like that again or I may have to get my dad on you.” She said laughing uncontrollably.

This was amazing just having to vent and exchange secrets. It was a plus to be talking with my crush all this time. Eventually, we went our separate ways and back to our homes. Mel was strangely at my house with his smirk. I just know he going to tell me something along the line of I told you so.

"What did Myra tell you, champ?" Mel asked me on my way into the doorway.

"Nothing. We just went for a jet ride and talk." I said.

"How can you be busy talking in the air like that? The speed didn't catch your tongue?" Mel asked me.

"We had it in neutral. Why you asking me all this anyway?" I asked irritable.

"I don't know, maybe just looking out for a friend I knew since a toddler while a robotic babysitter nearly raise the two of us. I just got a worried feeling about this one you're talking to." Mel said along with sarcasm.

"Her and I are not dating. We just have a tiny attraction to one another and hung out, bro. I can set you up with one of the girls in her group." I insisted.

"Really, you'll do that? Well, never mind me old friend or buddy ole pal. I'll just head home before it gets late." Mel said before hopping into the Sky Raiser.

Mel really into this Myra and I storyline which he somehow had planted in his head. I hope he finds someone to bother with all those questions. I may take the high road and stay to myself for a while. If he goes out the trust circle of this friendship, I'll have to leave him on no man's land. I'm just as reliable as these techno gadgets they keep springing up each year.

I turned to the news on my televised ceiling as I laid on my bed. I seen our first ever presidential robot in a press conference. I scratch my head at all the seriousness the press had for this metallic piece of junk. I'm certain all of them must've been that lonely kid and needed a robotic friend to overlook their flaws and ways. I'm quite judgmental, but that's not the whole side of me. Another side of me is quite considerate regardless what people around me may think.

On the other hand, I was amazed and certain that I had to break things off with Myra. A Race Through Time competition is now a statewide tournament and I was guaranteed a winning streak. With Mr. Blank being Myra's dad, I knew I had to play my cards right for my selected spot in the tournament.

I started thinking as my room turned into a shrine of mood colors: green was happy, red was upset, and blue was sadness. The colors on my walls went from red to blue, blue to red, and so on. I started getting light headed so I turned off Siri to cancel the room effect.

I came up with the perfect idea. I'll tell a white lie to ensure a spot in the tournament. I was confident that any beaming light won't slow me down during A Race Through Time.

Even though it seems messed up to tell my teacher I won't see his daughter anymore while in all actuality I will do the exact opposite, I knew that he would understand man to man. I rubbed my hands very tight ready for this plan to make way and take victory on such a loved sport.

Chapter 4-

A FEW SCREWS MISSING

It was finally career day on the shuttle and I was back in the class screaming in my head free at last. I was always a nerd for studies and inherited a funny laugh as well.

“Guess what, class? President Metal is coming to class to tell you all about leadership and perseverance. After all, those are the vocabulary words for the week.” Mrs. Mathews said with a huge grin.

“Wow, I had no idea his name would be metal.” I said sarcastic and proceed laughing.

“That’s enough, Jim. You’re just another example why I’m having Principal Aileen watch the back of the class while President Metal is presenting his role in the community.” Mrs. Mathews announced while I slumped down in my holographic chair.

“Why? Oh, why the horror? Two non humans babysitting a class of humans. This can’t be true.” Mel said jokingly as he surprisingly joined in.

He gave me a wink and it occurred that I haven’t talked to him in a week.

“Now class, we don’t tolerate discrimination however their outer appearance may be. That’s not what we do ever. We have grown far from that. You know there was even a time race was separated and even religion. I can go all day but I’ll save it for another lesson.” Mrs. Mathews ranted.

I raised my hand.

“Yes, Jim.” She said.

“Well, I’m actually excited to see President Metal. It sounds like you’re a big fan of robots.” I said making the class giggle.

“Yes he also have enough smarts as us humans. There’s no need to call him that name.” Mrs. Mathews said.

“Well, looks like you got the code of love all in your system ain’t it.” I said.

“That’s Enough, Jim!” Mrs. Mathews shouted.

“Sorry, I was just joking. No need to get all loud for the class.” I replied.

Mel looked at me confused as a deer in headlights.

“Why the long face, Mel? You want to appoligize, huh?” I asked him.

“Yes, Jim you may start by apologizing for all the interrupting you have been doing lately.” Mrs. Mathews said circling the attention back on me.

Interesting enough, I gave in and kept my mouth shut. No more interruptions will come out me and I meant it. I would rather get kicked out of the A Race Through Time competition than interrupt the class one more time.

Myra kept looking over at me. I made a snap and pointed toward her trying to flirt. She responded by blowing air kisses at me.

Mel raised his hand giving me a disappointed look as his eyes glared with his face red as a tomato.

“Mel, honey. Is everything alright with you?” Mrs. Mathews asked.

“Actually no, I’m not feeling too well.” He replied.

“I’ll let you head on out and get to our nurse pod straight ahead in the center of the ship.” Mrs. Mathews said as he was dismissed.

My face squinted and I felt a touch of suspicion to Mel’s cruel behavior lately. Why did he get so hot headed over Myra and I flirting? Is he liking her as well? Why didn’t he just say so instead making me think she was up to no good? The questions made my suspicion that much true and I was ready to call his bluff.

Mel returns and this time he was holding his stomach with both hands.

I was thinking he must’ve ate something he was allergic to. After all, his face did make an unusual bright reddish look and he’s currently having stomach problems. I know part of me is telling me to forgive him and forget the manipulating he’s been doing.

I also thought about earlier when Mrs. Mathews seen that book that was written long ago. I thought again and again maybe he has something similar, but I have not yet read this mysterious book.

I shortly raised my hand.

“Alright Jim, this isn’t an outburst. Is it?” Mrs. Mathews asked.

“No, I’m actually interested in that plague book you mentioned a while back.”

“Oh yes, I do have one copy with me. What made you so interested in that book?” She asked.

“No reason, I used to love medical stuff when I was a kid. The experience will sure bring that kid side out of me.” I said.

Mrs. Mathews grabs the book as it appeared right after clicking submit for request on her laptop. She told me to make sure she get it back after the school year is up.

I had the book in my hands and honestly felt normal than the rest of this world. Finally, no gadgets or glitches to occur and I can work on my reading without having to go up against a screen. I felt the joy pour over me like a waterfall.

Myra noticing me hugging the book like it was a baby.

“So adorable, you and that book. Wish that book was me.” She said making me smile hard.

Everybody else in the class could’ve cared less. Honestly, they didn’t want to see any paper and pencil. One guy named Borg think he was brought here specifically by technology and not from human beings themselves.

Borg must’ve thought he would be a fully-fledged cyborg taken into humanity. I laughed covering my mouth trying to not disrupt class. He acts like a cyborg trying to talk all robotic in slow phrases and he tries to act like lasers come out of his human skin. One day, he kept pointing at the teacher as she acted like she was getting laser shots.

I’m always going to be team paper and team pencil until the day I leave this earth. Technology typed efforts was okay for me, but I feel more accomplished writing my works instead of typing them. For instance, if there is someone see me typing they may mistake it as texting. That misunderstanding can cause a lot of attention away from the so called written work.

"Look at this cavemen holding a book. Look at who needs summer shuttle lessons." Borg said cracking up laughing.

He was the only person laughing throughout the whole space shuttle.

"Why is this one home shuttle in such a laughing mood?" Mrs. Mathews asked.

"Because this home shuttle have class comedians versus the class clowns." I said.

"Who are the class clowns, Jim?" Mrs. Mathews asked.

"Whoever showing up as President Metal and Principal Aileen." I explained.

"Very funny, Jim. Are you the clown?" Mrs. Mathews asked.

"Maybe. Is it safe to be a clown out here?" I asked.

"Is it safe to allow your rage at technology to take away others thirst for knowledge? I didn't think so." Mrs. Mathews said with her smile.

As we were dismissed for the day until we have to meet back in the space shuttle by late this afternoon, I notice Mel as I figure I patch things up with him. I missed my sky pal and the ultimate jokester himself.

"Listen man, I'm sorry for not speaking to you. It's just those comments and questions about Myra made me jittery inside. Honestly, I felt bad." I explained.

"You right bro. No hard feelings?" Mel asked.

"I can promise no hard feelings, but I'm still going to be a hard critic for all these brainiacs with a few screws missing." I said while he laughed.

He teared up and we shook hands coming to a complete understanding.

"You do know in that scenario you would be the brainiac while you're also saying they got a few screws missing. It's funny to think you can get by in life saying these crazy things." Mel replied.

"It's just venting, it's not suppose to make sense. Emotion is like a baby who doesn't know the right or wrong thing to say. Logic is like an adult who is supposed to be developed to understand right or wrong." I said while Mel mind was completely blown.

"You really smart bro. Them robots can't keep up with your witty logic no more than I could." Mel said thrilled.

"I'm having that three thousand logic worth billions in the future. It will take this place by storm." I said.

"Okay let's not get too hectic. We still have to see what we up against when President Metal enters the ship." Mel said.

"Oh yeah forgot about him. He look like your modern white president. It's sad we're now replacing all these man hard worked efforts in the same position as robots." I said as my eyes widen.

"They definitely will be turning in their graves, am I right Jim?" He asked.

"Yessir, that something I can definitely imagine. I feel like for the time being we should keep the opinions to ourselves. This robot scares me because I don't know a lot of its functions and battery powered malfunctions." I said.

"Yeah, I wouldn't worry about all that. Somebody can just pull his wires and he would shut down faster than a kid in a sugar coma." Mel said tickled.

Funny thing is, I never thought Mel and I would ever patch things up and still laugh like old times. I may not know everything that comes to mind. I do however can't see a robot taking my place. It may not matter what I think anyway the more we praise robotics like a national anthem or symbol.

It was almost six o'clock and everyone got on their suits and back into the home shuttle.

President Metal finally showed up as a cut on his chin showed part of him had been rewired. It was a revealing part of it circuit which seem a bit odd. He notices the class looking at it while he covers it with his right hand.

"Now. Students. You. Should. Never. Turn. Your. Back. On. School." President Metal slowly said one word after the next.

"Life. Is. Like. A. Box. Of. Chocolates. It. Is. Overly. Eaten. And. Yet. Tasty." President Metal said loudly and proudly.

Principal Aileen sat in the center toward the back of our home shuttle. She was clapping through small parts of President Metal speech. I kept getting a headache hearing the two sound like a uncoordinated band group. I laid my space helmet down on my holographic desk and went for a nice nap.

Mrs. Mathews this time didn't care if my peers slept along as nobody interrupted her precious president from his presentation toward us.

As I lifted my space helmet a few times, I notice Mel also had his head down and the insane clapping got on his nerves too. I just knew everyone in the class felt like saying something but don't want to get in trouble for discriminating a lab made robot and an alien found on earth. We gave them human titles and they are the least bit humans. I thought maybe President Metal or Principal Aileen aren't the ones with a few screws missing than my peers and Mrs. Mathews.

I went back down for another nap. As I slowly lowered my helmet downward, the whole class clapped their hands suddenly except for me.

"Come on now, let's give a hand for President Metal taking time out of his busy day to speak to us." Mrs. Mathews insisted while I rolled my eyes.

Principal Aileen did one of those Star Trek sign languages. Principal Aileen use to always say in the past the show helped her remember how home was like for her.

President Metal shortly walked stiff and almost stride out the back of the home shuttle.

“I know it’s getting late guys, so instead of dismissing you all. I’ll transport y’all back to each address. Ready? Have a good one, see you all next time!” Mrs Mathews said excitedly waving her remote over our heads pressing a button.

Everyone including me poof back into our hovering homes. Unlike the rest of them, I wasn’t impressed and it was more as I expected coming from an alien and robot.

My parents was smiling in the doorway. It seemed like they were filled with questions.

“It was okay I guess. Our principal sat with us. I don’t think President Metal said much.” I told my parents.

“He is a man of short words but a breath of fresh air.” My mom said smiling up at our ceiling.

However, my dad look concerned.

“Honey, what you mean by that?” He asked her.

“Nothing. I am just admiring a lot he has done for all of us. You need to read his digital book called A World Leader. It’s so good, hun.” She explained to my dad.

“What some wise robot going to say that humans have never said? There were humans before robots. Umm, Hello.” He said mocking my mom with a smirk.

“Stop arguing in front of our son. Terribly sorry kiddo you didn’t enjoy it and that your father and I almost got off topic. It happens with marriage, that’s all.” My mom said.

I went back to my room and hoped for another dream for my journal. It’s been a while since I took a dive in it. I must be getting like the rest of us powered by technology and almost losing my penmanship to digital creations.

I took a deep breath and instantly fell into a deep sleep.

The dream felt cloudy and my vision slowly derailed to a point I been squinting very hard.

"Where is everyone?" I asked in the dream.

I notice twenty dark shadows approaching me and it sounded like the voices of my parents. It felt like a robotic impression of my parents. At this point I knew I was dreaming self consciously, but I kept my eyes closed seeing what was next in this vivid dream.

I slipped into a puddle and the voices of my parents slowed down in a malfunction robotic manner. My vision reappeared back to normal and I see my parents. Instead of twenty figures, it was my exact two parents standing right in front of me.

They hugged me.

"We appoligize son. Thank you for saving us from mind controlled robots. I think we humans created a monster after all." My dad said rubbing my head.

After a blink, I woke up early that morning and sprinted for my journal.

Opening it once again, I decide to add to the front page of my journal.

The front page writes:

A world like today solved by the great scheme of world wars and politics. A world without devices and technological efforts. Those people took pride in their work enough to redo a draft or solve a problem.

It became my honest decision to make my dreams a reality through stopping technology from destroying our human race. My dream is the messenger and I am the deliverer through thick and thin.

I finished writing my daily journal entry and closed it right away. Since it was too early to be up right now, I went back to bed. Besides, I have a big day in the next few weeks.

"It's time to bring on the magic." I whispered to myself drifting off into a slumber.

Chapter 5-

A COMPETITION AGAINST ALL ODDS

For the next week, I trained with my bud Mel. We tried setting up an obstacle race in my front room. Mel trained me in the most imaginable way, he will have me run straight across the floorboards and point either saying fast or slow to get me ready for the competition. In this case scenario, Mel would be the lightning beam pushing me either in slow motion or sped up motion.

"Fast!" He shouted like a Drill Sargent.

I sped up like a rocket into the sky. Then, I dodge as if laser beams were firing me down in that direction. Finally, I crossed the finish line represented by the electric chimney in my living space.

"Wow, that was quick Jim." He said giving me the thumbs up.

We did a few exercises from push ups to sit ups to running in place.

"Nice, let's sky jump this thing into fifth gear kiddo." I said using todays lingo.

"That's right bro. By the way, how you and Myra doing?"

"Doing just fine now that I got a plan to secure my spot in A Race Through Time." I replied.

"You don't think you getting a bit ahead of yourself?" He asked me.

"No, I do not think I am. Take a wild guess of whose the father of Myra." I insisted.

“Wait, is it?” He asked and paused in the middle of his question.

I nodded my head silently giving him a yes instead of no.

“What? Mr. Blank is her father. I don’t even see the resemblance.” Mel said.

“I didn’t either but it’s true. I heard some awful things about his love interest.”

“Eww, how would you know that?” Mel asked.

“From Myra, Mel. Try to catch up now.” I said.

“I’m caught up. I think.” He said looking up at the ceiling.

The pause occurring was so very awkward I started shouting out for no apparent reason. Mel had to quiet me down with his yelling. We were like two pit bulls barking at one another.

“You’re crazy, man. Let’s continue this training though.” I said.

“Not so fast, bro. Tell me more how this Myra thing is connected with your spot in the big race.” Mel said.

After each question, I realize he is just like me feening for more information after our last conversation. That quality I can respect from Mel and know we’re strengthening our young minds each year. I finally told him my big plan with Myra and her father. I can trust him to not spill the beans out to anybody on that ship leading up to the big competition.

"That's tough. I'm all for it. I can be your cover up instigator if you want bro." Mel said chuckling.

"Why would I need someone like that? I hope my cover not too blown that I will need someone to tell a lie on top an already bigger lie!" I exaggerated.

"Is it lying though? I know deep down how you feel about Myra. You're just trying to tell a white lie to make everyone happy, that's all." Mel said.

I was tempted to feed into his insane logic that surprisingly made more sense after the sweat on my face cooled off. Mel must've underestimated Myra's dad's protectiveness of her daughter and his thing with robots. I tried to just go along with it for the sake of arguing.

"Great minds think alike and you my friend have opened my eyes to an even bigger plan." I said.

"Okay sure." Mel said with a smirk.

He knew what I was saying about my plan was too good to go exactly as I wanted it to go. I disregard that notion and went on to him about another plan besides lying to Mr. Blank and nearly jeopardizing my spot in the competition.

From what I heard recently, A Race Through Time competition takes place on one of the motherships that span as far and wide as a pro golf field. There were a bunch of room for candidates to run as fast as our legs can manage. The bleachers sat out like first class plane seats. It was told to always have seats packed with nearly eighty thousand civilians and half of them are robots. The world I'm living in might be weird and insanely advanced, but I was loving every bit of excitement for this main event.

“Nice chatting with you! I have to go help my dad fix the electric microwave. It’s jammed in our wall, so it stops food from being zapped completely.” Mel said soon before exiting onto the Sky Raiser.

I walked toward my bedroom to watch some programs on my televised ceiling.

This cowboy show was on and it was the most interesting thing. Their world seemed so peaceful and less robotic as everyone moved wildly across the Great Plains. I thought to myself this had to be almost a thousand years back and maybe even more.

There were two ranchers who were hunting some cattle and got in attack mode with one another. Bam! Bam! Click, Clack, Boom! The noises of gun fire and explosions blast through the sound waves in my room. My bed even motioned as if I was on the saddle of a horse. The motion went up and down like getting off a bumpy ride.

“Wow!” I exclaimed.

I went for my dream journal once more and on these few pages I drew grass with lines marking the wind, sun, and a rancher from the show. I wanted to outline the simpler times. This journal was a ticket to another world simpler and breath taking. It clicked in my head about how I want to change all that. I wanted to remind every single body, robot, and even Principal Aileen that times used to be simpler and you don’t have to stress out over screens and holograms.

There was nothing stopping me now but a white lie and natural born confidence. I stepped firmly at my door making a salute to the imaginary people in the walls of my bedroom. I know this sounds a bit self absorb, but I call it a new version of me. The new improve Jim and that was going to be my motto for the rest of the year three thousand.

I had a lot of energy this time of night and I took the jet pack and refilled every ounce of it. I tip toed that night out the door while my parent slept.

The jet pack seem light carrying in the dark. I look down at it and it was destroyed.

"Who can destroy something so magically made in a way humans can take their own flight through the sky?" I wondered.

I held my chin and thought maybe I slept walk the night before forgetting I ever broke the jet pack. I know Mel is going to have a fit and his dad as well. I planned on throwing it outside my door since the house is hovering pretty high above waste of nearly eighty years.

This was only a minor setback, but let's hope this is the only set back I have from this point on.

The night was young and I decided to double down on my journal writing goals for next year. I was a bit of an goodie two shoes or an over achiever if you ask me.

The journal writes:

Goals for 3001

- *Become a Pro Athlete*

- *Create a Time Machine*

- *Live on Mars*

• *Create New Opportunity*

I knew most of those I can soon accomplish as long as I stick with this competition in high hopes Mel never spills the beans of this plan.

The next day, I was in hopes to have a talk with my parents. They went out on a date and by date I mean going to different rooms and holographically meeting up with each other. Their holograms were like blue pixels of their dispersed image spewing in the eyes of one another. I don't know if they ever made up after their last fight and trying to stay strong with one another for my sanity.

Crazy how life works in mysterious ways. I'm the only one that has something healthy with a love interest and not knee deep in bitterness or hatred.

"No biggie." I said flying up the Sky Raiser on a beautiful Sunday.

I was right there on the doorstep of Myra place. The only issue was keeping her and I a secret from her dad. She was looking stunned at me for not calling before swinging by her brick home. She moved to the side and out appears an angry man being my gym teacher Mr. Blank.

"Jim, what exactly are you doing here? Shouldn't you be training for this competition?" Mr. Blank asked with his arms folded.

Shucks, I got caught in my ways and was stumbling over my words.

"Honestly, I would like to take Myra out to a nice restaurant hovering in the city." I told Mr. Blank.

"No, she has a lot of chores around the house." He said.

"Don't we have robots for that?" I asked.

"What's that, son? Do I hear back talk from somebody asking to take my daughter out in the sky?" He asked me as my legs quivered.

"No. No sir. I would never cross that line. My parents raised me right and I will love to prove that." I said feeling like my character was questioned.

"Yes. In matter of fact, step inside as we all have a little talk." He said.

"Sure. Thank you for being so cool and letting me join the competition!" I exclaimed.

"No problem, kid." He said giving me a pat on the back.

We all sat on the glistening couch that changed any color as your mood varied.

"Woah, this couch is nice. It must be very new and expensive." I said amazed.

"Nope, it was on sale. I used my virtual coins I saved a while back." Mr. Blank said.

"Smart man." I said.

"You're a good kid, but I know you know my little secret about robots. I love them. They are the most wonderful partners you can bring into this world." He said as our heads turned.

"You don't think that's a bit strange, sir. No defense to your liking, but humans got the same qualities." I said.

"Yes, you're right. How about I have Myra tell you her liking in all actuality?" He asked.

"No." Myra said.

"She mean that she don't want to talk about it now and she needs time to think it over." Mr. Blank said toward me.

"No dad, I'm saying I been crushing on Jim for a while now. I just need time to process you and mom separation. What a robot got that mom doesn't?" Myra asked after standing up to her dad.

"Well, let's think. Oh yeah, they have an off button in case things get snappy and they feel like fussing." He said.

He was a little embarrassed seeing her reaction ending in tears and hugged her very tight.

"Sweetie, it's something I'm going through. I don't want you to think you're responsible for this. After all, you're the best thing out of me and your mom marriage." Mr. Blank said as I start to head out of such a beautiful moment.

"Jim, where you going?" He asked me.

"Umm, I don't want to ruin the moment. Those speeches y'all said to each other were beautiful." I said.

"Well, I can see your parents sure did raise you the right way. You can take out my daughter before it gets late. Don't mess this up before the big race in a couple of weeks." Mr Blank said slowly letting go of his hug from Myra.

Myra grabbed my hand as she released from her father's hug. Her eyes gleamed ready to have some fun.

We took the Sky Raiser over to Kicking Chicken which was a floating restaurant and the most electronic restaurant ever made. The Kicking Chicken had food zapped by the push of a button only the employees used. Zapping food to your table took a lot of waitress/ waiters jobs even the robotic ones. I had enough virtual change to take both Myra and I orders.

"Hey, Welcome to the Kicking Chicken! This is the future and we take pride in a zap away! What can I get for you?" The voice box greeted and asked us while we search the digitalize menu.

"What you think about getting, Myra?"

"I think about getting the number 5. That looks so good."

"That does look delicious, I'll try it as well. A chicken tender salad with ranch sauce alongside a medium sweet tea. You can make two orders of this meal as well please and thank you." I said amongst the voice box.

Myra looked at me blinking simultaneously. Her eyes changed a different color and seemed a bit less human the more my sight of her raise suspicion. As food zapped to our plates, her stomach growled and sounded like construction work all in her stomach. I began to reminisce all the way through our time together.

"Myra, what's that crunched up noise?" I asked.

“It almost sound like a garbage disposal or crushed up metal parts.” I added.

“I have to come clean about something. The reason I have been so wired to you is through my dad. I’m a cyborg that’s half female half robot. I’m sorry if I offend you in any way.”

“Offend me how? This is my life.” I said.

“Your life? How about how I’m living?” Myra questioned.

“A privilege cyborg and or daughter sent to bait me all along, because their parent is obsessed with loving robots.”

“Why are you so judgmental?”

“Don’t try that emotional thing with me? Robots don’t have emotion.” I said.

“They sure don’t, but cyborgs do.” Myra explained.

“They do?” I asked.

“Yes. The robot that my dad divorced my mom was actually my biological robotic mother. It’s a weird thing I’m having with my identity crisis. Do I want to be full human or full machine mode?” She asked herself.

“Well, I’m just in luck with all the surprises. It seems like my life is scripted and less enjoyable. What’s next you’re going to tell me? My results in the A Race Through Time Competition!” I exclaimed to Myra while she was crying trying to look away.

“You are a good man. I just want you to accept me.” Myra said to me.

"Wait, is that why we had that talk with your dad and he wanted you to speak out about something? Is that why your dad is so protective and want a guy that loves robots just like he does?"

"Yes, I think. The last part I'm not sure what my dad intentions are." Myra said.

"Well I accept you just the way you are. I don't think my parents will have any problem with you whatsoever. They already pressuring me to be a whiz with techno gadgets anyway." I said trying to make a joke.

"Hahaha." Myra laughed as one drip of sweat traveled down her forehead.

"Don't need to be nervous. I'm not upset. You're still the gorgeous thing I laid eyes on. Cyborg, okay. There's no wonder why you look so human. You are human and the great invention of mankind." I said slowly becoming interested.

Chapter 6-

RETURN TO SENDER

"Wait a minute, that's music to my ears. A dude who absolutely hate technology is dating a cyborg girl made of half human cells and half wired motor parts. That is hysterical." Holographic Mel said jokingly.

"Yeah no joke. I'm battling with myself at this point." I said with a sigh.

"I say go for it. It may lighten up your mind about gadgets and robots. You might have more respect for the year three thousand after all." Holographic Mel said making the bit of sense.

"You know the more you talk, the smarter things get out here. You may be a genius after all." I said smirking at his last comment.

"Thanks bro. You may be one after this revenge over the killer robots routine." Holographic Mel said laughing before I ended the call.

The stakes were high and I told myself I won't let any of these secrets get me off my game in the race. I'm going to train long and hard before Myra's secret and even the world get to me and my motivation to win. It was time to bring home the bacon and get the cash prize once and for all. It was nearly a week before the big competition and now I strictly only eat protein.

I only ate eggy white shakes for breakfast and steak for dinner. I was treating my body like a mean lean money making machine which I will gain that title after winning this competition.

"Jim, honey. You know I can scramble those eggs for you." My mom said at the dinner table.

"You know what Jim, I adore that you found something you're good at. Promise me you won't go overboard to get strong for this Race Through Time contest." My mom said shortly after thinking things over.

"You mean competition?" I asked correcting her word choice.

"Yes my mistake. Wise Guy." She said jokingly.

At this point, I feel like Wise Guy should just be my nickname since that's what everyone calls me when I correct them.

"You know I'm just kidding, Jim. You are my only child." My mom said smiling while pinching my cheek.

"I'm too old for that, but thanks for the compliment, mom." I said.

"You never too old unless they create an age tranquilizer. Shoot you right in the face as your face starts to mold both much older or younger. Man, I got to write these ideas down." My mom said proudly.

"Okay, I'm glad this conversation got you in a cheery mood." I told my mom leaving my bedroom window for school.

The ship was filled with robotics. It was a day we learned to operate robots around us. We got so use to them in the year three thousand that in case of an emergency we treat them like any human.

"Good Morning, Mrs. Mathews! How wonderful it's like in the ship I so wonderfully love?" I greeted and asked myself in a jolly mood.

"Well, glad to see you turned a new leaf. Good job! I never been so proud of you than now, Jim." Mrs. Mathews said while we went for the space suits.

"Look who's finally getting use to life on the spaceship." Mel said loving the switch in me.

I walked in and subconsciously sat next to Myra thrilled to learn and admire her beauty. I had a lot of questions for her as a cyborg, but was too hesitant to ask in the fear of freaking her out.

"Hey lovely." I said to her while she waved and looked back at Mrs. Mathews.

"Woah, everything alright or did I hit your ware and tear?" I said laughing and slamming the desk.

She kept a straight face until giving out a snort and laugh.

"Okay you got me. I just had this long talk with my parents and it's been non stop arguing. I just can't with them no more." Myra told me.

"Good thing you can talk with your folks, communication is like a rare species in my household. You may only see once or twice." I exaggerated.

Mrs. Mathews lasers a hole in my seat and I fell to the ground of the home shuttle.

“I didn’t want to do it this time Jim. This is nearly the last of the marking period and I need you guys to focus.” Mrs. Mathews reminded us.

“Yes ma’am.”

“No it is yes Mrs. Mathews. Age is nothing but a number.” Mrs. Mathews said.

“Okay I stand corrected. Yes, Mrs. Mathews.” I replied.

The class enjoyed some of my outburst and thought it was the most interesting than any material the class heard all year. Mel smiled and sat next to Myra friend Liz. We kids got so tired of these space suits we started designing it with digital paintings and we have videos covering our entire suits. I’m the only one without the digital decorated space suits being I never want to blend in with the crowd.

“Now students when you boarded the ship, what did you guys see and how it made you feel? Anyone?” Mrs. Mathews asked.

I raise my hand.

“I see more robots than usual and it may me feel willing to learn more about them.” I chimed into the conversation.

“Correct, today students we’re going to take a closer look at robotics such as what they eat, drink, and their metal parts in case some of you would like to be nurses or doctors one day.” Mrs. Mathews said as everyone eyes grew wide under their space helmets.

Mrs. Mathews brought to the class a metal square piece with barb wires. I never been so terrified in my life like what if I get a shock from touching the side of the wire or even all of the wires.

Considering neither student touched the metal object with barbed wire, Mrs. Mathews felt it with the gloves of her suit to show that there was no harm when you come in close contact with it.

"See kids, nothing is going to harm you as long as you don't hold it with your bare hands. It's highly mandatory that you all follow this instruction." Mrs. Mathews said.

I took out my hand to be the first person to try feeling this metallic piece and barbed wire.

"Great. Thanks Jim for participating!" Mrs. Mathews exclaimed.

"My pleasure." I said.

"Such a gentleman." Myra said as I walked back to my holographic chair.

"That's sweet of you Myra to compliment your classmate." Mrs. Mathews said.

Class was a blast and by blast I mean quick as anybody could blink. Mrs. Mathews taught us how to compare motor parts to human organs. In case of an emergency, we would be capable to help our fellow robot in no time.

There was a specific robot out on the front end of the ship. She had a wig attached to her and bright lipstick on her Artificial Intelligence lips.

"Myra, how have you been hun?" The robot asked.

"Mom, I want you meet Jim. I met him in Mrs. Mathews home shuttle. Her class do get quiet really quick when Jim starts spewing his logic."

"Awe that is so sweet, mister. My name is Robotica the second and I was made in Switzerland way back."

"Oh well that's nice. I heard Switzerland got lovely inventions created." I said making small talk.

"Is this a first time thing dating a cyborg?" Robotica asked being a bit nosy.

"Yes. It's some getting use to, but we all human some shape or form. Am I right?" I asked hoping to reason well with Mrs. Robotica.

Robotica was great at helping with oil machinery and I had no idea she works the ship from sunrise to sun down. Mr. Blank came in swaying across the platform and gave Robotica a kiss on the cheek.

"Come on mom and dad. Get a room at least." Myra said trying to block it out of her memory.

"How does memory operate as a cyborg anyhow?" I asked.

"It must be the same as any robot, but for me memory goes in and out sometimes due to half human and half robotic brain. It just comes with being one." Myra replied.

"That must be hard." I said.

"No, not really. I don't feel pain at all." Myra said chuckling.

"That's nice." I said.

Myra grabbed my hand as we walked with her mother and Mr. Blank. Mrs. Robotica was in actuality a five foot robot who look identical to a white blond hair girl with bright lipgloss. I was amazed at its Artificial Intelligence graphics.

In the middle of admiring her physical makeup, I had to cool myself down before I be too much like Myra's dad Mr. Blank.

"So Jim, I wanted to inform you that we added something extra for the competition next week. You won't just go up against human specimens, but also any size or form." He said not trying to offend Mrs. Robotica or Myra.

"Wait, by shape or form do you mean robots and stuff?" I asked after Mr. Blank tries to silence me from offending our ladies.

"Son. Yes, that is what I'm referring to." Mr. Blank explained trying to keep it subtle.

"You know we robots aren't that easily offended, right? Let's just all relax and enjoy the tour." Mrs. Robotica informed Mr. Blank and I.

"Well, it seems we got a lot to learn you and I, Jim." Mr. Blank said.

"Yes sir." I replied.

After we said our goodbyes, I was teleported back to my home ready to workout for the rest of the day. I'm trying to get as buff and strong as those robots. Robots could even crush concrete which was fascinating learning it in class. I never thought I'll have an interest in techno things like robots and teleportation.

I did nearly one hundred sit-ups in five sets. I was destined to work on my abdomen and torso. The amount of air in my lungs was breathing out like a blow torch. I began to think if I needed more gadgets to keep my legs from slowing down during the competition, but my conscious considers it cheating.

Win or lose, I knew I was at least good at something other than the journals I wrote every day. I got a cool cyborg girl love interest and even set my friend Mel up with Liz. Come to think of it, they may all be cyborgs just hanging out with one another.

I put on the second jet pack going out once more. At this point, I think Mel's extra jet pack might as well have been a birthday gift since I kept it this long. Even though he never told me it being a gift from him, he may have figured I would come to that conclusion on my own.

I was flying high and high seeing mothers earth from the sky view. It was like seeing crush up lava plants around and around. It was a very toxic place to still have houses upon in year three thousand. I have to just imagine walking on it through television programs on my ceiling and can't be too worried since I was born into this generation.

"Let's get it started in here." I sang remembering that old song from my great ancestors.

Singing and jet pack flying was a must on my bucket list I can officially cross off completely. I smiled hard until each cheek on my face glisten to a bright red.

I was finally back at home putting up my jet pack after having some relief in the sky facing every drop of fear inside me.

Unfortunately, our teacher Mrs. Mathews sent a hologram of her coughing and sneezing. I was really looking forward to our next class on the ship. I was told to stay home and practice giving a robot the Heimlich Maneuver.

I simply traveled to Myra's place in the Sky Raiser. I think I'm making quite the impression on her parents. She notice me through the tube of the Sky Raiser and I landed uncontrollably in their living room not noticing the door all the way open.

"Everything okay? You landed kind of hard." Myra said concerned for dear life.

"Kid, you good?" Mr. Blank asked me walking right into my fall.

"Yes, I'm fine." I said.

"I had a plan up my sleeve, Myra. Let's talk in private about this coming competition." I said forgetting her dad was in the other room.

"I plan on using gadgets to help me through the competition." I told Myra.

"I don't think you should be telling me that. I keep information confidential the best way I know how depending on who's near." Myra warned me.

"I thought your dad went in the other room." I said.

"Yep but our walls are still thin and he can hear you. You are at serious risk for predetermined disqualification." Myra said mocking her cyborg voice.

The tinted screen door slid automatically into the other space of the wall and there was Mr. Blank disappointed that I would think of something so devious.

"You can forget that spot in the competition and why you think you need gadgets to win anyhow?" He asked while his face turned red.

"Please, give me a second chance. I will come early to set everything up if you like." I begged.

"Tempting to the point I'll think it over. You two keep it down. Mrs. Robotica is sleeping." He said.

That was the very first time I seen Mr. Blank put on his authority voice and became so stern. I was impressed and like the way he cared for a robotic artificial intelligence wife. Somebody from a thousand years back would have seen this and completely black out immediately.

"My dad is right though, Jim. In fact I want to help you train for the competition." Myra insisted.

The partnership was set and Myra wanted to help me by cooking for me until the start of the competition. I already weighed at least one hundred and seventy pounds. These robots weighed more so it may just slow them down even with a laser beam to give them that assistance.

The very next day I met back at Myra's house and her parents were out somewhere. We set up a obstacle race around her house. We race a few laps over and spent the rest of the day to run out for some smoothies at a hovering store through the Sky Raisers. There were literally tubes that would get you one place to the next. It was like a getting sucked through a vacuum and coming out the other end in a totally new destination.

"What smoothie would you like?" I asked Myra.

"The nutty professor smoothie. You should try it if you not allergic to any peanuts or bananas." She said in the line of the store.

"Nope not allergic to any of those things." I said.

"Good, would you want one too. I got my dad's virtual coin grab." Myra said as I nodded.

A virtual coin grab was a holographic card that when you slide it your information of your pin goes automatic in the cashier system without revealing any sensitive information from the next person.

Myra also informed me that I should wear my spacesuit as I come in early on the mothership to help set up with her dad. She told me good luck and make sure I let bygones be bygones by the end of the race.

"Yes, I will definitely keep good sportsmanship under my belt." I said while she leaned in for a hug.

Chapter 7-

TWO WORLDS COMBINED IN ONE

I called up Mel in a hologram and this time sent myself in hologram mode as well. It was sort of like a modern FaceTime call. Instead of camera being on and off, the option is holograph on or off at a push of a button.

"How things been man? Is everything going according to plan?" Mel hologram asked.

"Yes and yes. Almost blew my cover trying to expose the big plan to shut down every robot and machinery at this big event." I said.

"Woah, are you not afraid you'll get in trouble?" Mel asked.

"Well, I been doing my digital research and notice the last person that tried to extinct robots got sent back a thousand years."

"A thousand years? How come that hasn't been brought to the likes of others?" Mel asked.

"It's government and confidential. President Metal said it can be dangerous to open it to the entire world." I explained.

"What does he know anyhow? His species is dangerous to the entire world. There's even movies of him as a villain sent to destroy humanity. Now this wise robot a leader of our nation. It's crazy." My holographic self ranted.

"I get it bro. Maybe you should rethink your plan. Did you think about Myra and her supposedly mother."

"How you know her mom?" I asked

"Everyone knows Robotica. Like I said in the past, you have been so focus on stopping technology a lot in your life that everything that shouldn't be new to you seems new. I get it that we have an objective for people to let go of gadgets, but instead of wiping it out completely there should be baby steps and small measures taken to prevent chaos." Holographic Mel said while his speech had me in complete silence.

"So what you're saying is baby steps needs to be taken?" I questioned.

"Yes, just think about it and give me a ring when you get the chance. Good luck on the race! I'll be out there to support." Mel said ending the call.

Mel's hologram strangely stayed still in the dead center of my bedroom. The lights had a sensor on it that set off an alarm sounding oddly like white noise.

"Hey Mel, you still there? Did I end the call right on my end?" I asked.

His hologram stayed in a waved stance.

Suddenly, his finger bent down and slowly the pixels dismantled itself as the real Mel himself poured out of the blue coated pixelated image in front of me.

"I'm just messing with you bro. I can now go through holograms with my actual body. I just wanted to show you the upgrade I got on my gadget. I better be on my way out now for real this time. Good luck out there bro." Mel said leaving my bedroom laughing.

What on mother kryptonite was that? This technology gets stranger and stranger. At first I thought the call froze his body up and he was a goner. I guess I got some adjusting to do after that long talk with Mel. Let me think, I could jot down a speech to tell everyone at the competition and include an announcement about remembering simpler times like year one thousand or two thousand.

My mind wondered off and soon it came back to me. I will include a speech and tie it to the crowd. First, I wanted to at least weigh myself into modern books and books dated back to almost a thousand years.

There was one person who mentioned a book dated for 2020 titled: The Plague That Started It All. As I thought more on the term plague, I realized it must've done a lot of harm to people in that time.

I decided to have a talk with my teacher who's not feeling as well. I called her up on my fancy holographic watch.

Mrs. Mathews's hologram stood three inches tall over my wrist extremely exhausted.

"Why are you calling me at this hour, Jim? Everything going alright?" Holographic Mrs. Mathews asked.

"I wanted to let you know I started the book and am fascinated by it. How did you hear about it?" I said and asked Mrs. Mathews hologram.

"I had it passed down through generations in my family. The book was a lovely perception before we got this advanced as a world." Holographic Mrs. Mathews said.

"Interesting. Now I think about it, you did tell us that in class a while back." I said.

"Indeed." Holographic Mrs. Mathews said.

Mrs Mathews shortly sneezed and little dust-like pixels fell to the ground.

"I will have it back to you in about a week, Mrs. Mathews." I said smiling reassuring she will have it back in time.

"Good, I'm hoping to hear your thoughts when you're finished with it. Enjoy your break and I hope to get over this cold." Holographic Mrs. Mathews said.

"Got it. Thanks, Mrs. Mathews! Get well soon!" I exclaimed with a huge smile.

"You're welcome. In the meantime, I'll see you whenever I see you. Good night, Jim!" Mrs. Mathews replied as she coughed and her hologram dispersed.

The book was red and showed a map on the front cover. The words from the title: A Plague That Started It All were spread out in all caps. The author with the pen name of Jamel Rogers was right below the title. The book was actually published in 2022 but judging by its summary the content is covering 2020's plague of a disease called Covid-19. It sounded like it had the whole world in an official lockdown as I read.

I sat and read as if it was the best experience to ever witness. I kept nodding while touching such an antique from way way back and skimming through chapter one in its entirety. I was even surprised that there was still cellphones during their time. I noted in my head that even zapping food have not been created during the early two thousands. I wonder when that start becoming a thing.

I went back to the old dream journal.

The next available page wrote:

NAME: JIM / DATE: 5/03/3000 / DREAM JOURNAL

Times were subtle with endless reminders of no return. As I read this book "The Plague That Started It All", I picture my world becoming like an empty pit of up to a third of the population ideas all in one. The way history worked blew my mind to smithereens. I felt like I had kryptonite and less human the more the day went by.

It was at this moment I knew exactly what I wanted most out of this world and the way the world was before or after technology.

I wanted TWO WORLDS COMBINED IN ONE!

I closed my dream journal and went to bed knowing in two days I have to prove myself. No more complaints and no more side comments. I'm starting to get use to this new opportunity of respecting the world of high tech and the world of old fashion way of living.

The next day came in a jiffy. I was up doing twenty push ups and twenty sit ups even before school that morning. We were on the ship in our suits as usual and I was sweating like someone poured a entire bucket of water above me. Mel noticed me and his eyes widen surprised.

"Yeah it's hot in this suit!" I exclaimed.

"Not anymore bro. I have a stamped filter that can add coolness to the suit if you need it."

"Yes, thanks Mel! That would do the job." I said relieved.

"What happened to you last night, Jim?"

"Oh nothing stayed up watching my televised ceiling. I think I may have a problem with being addicted to a cowboy rancher show."

"Try again. I know when you're lying like a court attorney." Mel said waiting for my response.

"Okay, I read up on a book that's been dated since 2022." I said.

"2022? You may need to slide a copy for me. I may read it as well." Mel said.

"I can't because somebody lend it to me and apparently it's a family tradition that they passed it on to their immediate family." I said to Mel.

"Why they give it to you then?"

"Who knows? They may just knew I was to be trusted and had good intentions no matter how blindly they see my arguments with the world today."

"Instead of world, you may want to start saying destruction. I heard we may not have another thirty years ahead of us." Mel warned.

"Where did you hear that?" I asked.

"The news. Do you ever watch the news?" Mel asked.

"Nope." I replied.

“You should, it keep us alert so no devastating series of events keeps on happening.” Mel added.

“I bet President Metal don’t know how to feel, because a robot can’t feel like a cyborg can.” I chimed.

The next day, we were back to our home shuttle for class. Mrs. Mathews turns at us with excited news.

“Kids, class is almost done with for the school year. Make sure you all get your parents to meet with the team either holographically or physical meet ups. I also will have Principal Aileen share remarks with you all.” Mrs. Mathews said while most students stared off in space.

Mel raised his hand and my attention darted in his direction. A range of emotion came across my facial expressions at Mel anticipating if he about to say something smart or spill out my previous plan.

“Jim, you want to step out for me?” Mrs. Mathews asked trying to see why my spacesuit sweating out a puddle at my very feet.

Mrs. Mathews took a deep breath shortly after I denied her request.

“Don’t tell me no. You can tell your peers that they lives must’ve not matter to you since you let a puddle sit under you without grabbing anything.

Myra wrote on a paper and stuck it on her space helmet with magnetic tape. It stuck like nail in a stud of a wall.

The paper reads:

Oh Jim, most handsome man! You challenge others way of thinking and so on.

On a serious note: I really want to study your conscious and one day be your support on this plan you have going on. We can play good cop bad cop or even do reverse psychology on those naysayers.

I was thrilled at her message and gave little message of my own. I stood up in the middle of class while even Mrs. Mathews looked at me like a ghost.

I decide to take Myra up on that offer and tried to set sometime after school to help her form her questions for me. I just hope some of these questions aren't too personal that it may offend her.

Across from her as I stood, I gave her a nod and thumbs up to show how serious I was taking the idea of her and I combined into one couple.

"Sit down, Jim. This isn't some love factory and you are not a love doctor so take a load off and sit." Mrs. Mathews said sternly.

"Got it. This your class and I am the student." I said sinking back into my holographic work area.

"Thank you for your cooperation, Jim. It means a lot." Mrs. Mathews responded.

I learned that today our lesson involves facing the fact that robots have natural thoughts and feeling like humans. I swear they make anything a lesson nowadays when a lot of this stuff people discuss everyday.

Mel hand raised a second time.

"If robots have feelings, can they feel when water touches them?"

"Yes, that's sort of like you touching an exposed wire. You will be stung so hard with electric circuits and be zapped into a hospital bed. That's how robots feel if you splash water all over them." Mrs. Mathews explained.

"Even as a practical joke?" Mel asked.

"What do you think, Mel?" She asked.

"Yes." Mel replied.

"Right on, any other questions?" Mrs. Mathews asked.

"How come we never learned about time machines?" I asked after my hand immediately raised.

"No one knows much about them except an early president of the late twenty eight hundreds. He died trying to test it out in front of his lab team."

"How come?"

"Good question. I guess some things aren't meant to be invented. Time is precious. Enjoy it while you still have time and not endless hope such as the desire to extend or back trace certain events." Mrs. Mathews said and teared up.

I clapped my hands as the half of the room began doing the same. That was such a teachable moment that Albert Einstein himself would have to give her that title. I can tell the half of my side of the room shuttle was making our teacher blush from cheek to cheek as out of it came a huge grin.

“Wow, that’s a new and lovely ending to the school year. Thank you for that wonderful round of applauses! I adore this class very much even when y’all get a bit rowdy at times.” Mrs. Mathews said giggling.

The doors pry open and a mist spew out in a thick fog into the class. Luckily, everyone had their helmets on so the fog doesn’t get in their eyes, nose, or mouth. Soon as the fog cleared, our appeared Principal Aileen. I knew I was going to miss that creature the least of all. Something about her being laid back tells me she’s plotting something. If I was her coming to a land of new species, I would feel terrified or even a bit worried.

“Hey, Principal Aileen.” The class said in a grumpy sigh and tone.

“Well specimens, I will let you all in on a secret. I may be retiring soon and heading back to my home planet. I had plans to leave this earth once and for all. Three words you all should live by.” Principal Aileen said while her eyes grew out of her sockets.

“Always expect extinction.” Aileen said creating suspicion from everyone.

Gasp came across the room and Mrs. Mathews was furious at her last three words. She was pushing the two eyed green terrestrial out the door. Soon, she tried coming back with a growl until the teacher used her zapping tool to blast her back to the home planet.

I nearly had a heart attack from the start of this paranoia. I didn’t expect it to be so bold about extinction.

"I'm sorry guys. The school need to do better at hiring roles on the ship." Mrs. Mathews said while we looked at her grunting.

"How you guys think about having a few days off and it will kick off the start of you guys summer?" She added while all of our eyes widen tremendously.

"Hooray to that!" I exclaimed before handshaking Mel behind me.

"Oh Jim, one other thing, remember your competition is coming up. You may need one other partner for it of your choosing. Mr. Blank will blow the whistle at the start of you and your partner's race." Mrs. Mathews said adding one small detail.

I began to think more and more as I realize the person for the job. That person is no other than my long term bud Mel. He will be an ultimate participant in the competition even if I haven't seen him run a obstacle just yet. I have enough faith in this team to hold victory.

Chapter 8-

THE BIG PRO AND CON

Mel was over at my house for two days and the competition was set after those days. I haven't seen him run anything these two days. I even tried to get him running and now figure out I was doing more than he usually does. I laughed at the fact he was a strict trainer to work with.

I slept long and hard that whole night before the big event of A Race Through Time. As early as nine o'clock in the morning, I was set to meet Mr. Blank in the mothership of all space shuttles. Each shuttle supported either offices or schools. The mothership supported things like stadiums or big commercial events.

I zapped myself into the mothership ready to get my hands dirty and take a look at the obstacles I was working toward in the race. Mr. Blank seen me and smiled with a brief nod. He asked me to follow him in the ticket booth just noticing how virtual reality it was.

"My friend, I want you to handle the tickets coming in like rapid fire. I'll cue you in when the competition starts. For now, can you sweep up any trash out on the platform to make sure there's no chance of injury." Mr. Blank asked wanting a favor.

"Sure, where would you like me to start?" I asked Mr. Blank.

"Anywhere you like." Mr. Blank said.

"Okay I'll start in the dead center and work my way outward." I replied.

"Thanks my guy! Keep up the good work." Mr. Blank said.

I went to the dead center and swept brushing every piece of metal, virtual coin reader, tranquilizers, and other devices. It felt great dumping all it in the trash. I see the tiny metal objects as therapeutic to my sanity against technology.

"Jim!! I'm going to give you more people to help! No rush!!" Mr. Blank yelled over at me.

"Thank you sir!" I shouted across the mothership.

I swept and swept. After an hour, I finally got toward the outer ring of the track it lit up as I stepped firmly on it. I was shocked.

As time slowly settled, we had two more hours before crunch time begins and participants shows up. Mr. Blank brought back two Artificial Intelligence robots over to help me clean. According to Mr. Blank, they'll have this whole circular track clean in five to ten minutes.

Mr. Blank looked over at me and was surprised to tell me about the new suits he picked up the other day. They were almost like track suits and it was all black separate by LED colors ranging from red, green, orange, and purple. I was the first one to get to select my suit I went with the red one cause it matched my shoe.

At last, Mel came aboard and on his way in selected a red glistening track suit. I was amazed at how much they put in to A Race Through Time game, because I haven't played it since a while back before now.

"You ready for the main event?" I asked Mel.

"I sure am. We're going to dust the track with these competitors."

Our competitors gradually boarded the ship and even some of the audience appeared out in the seats surrounding us. I notice a specific non human from the audience other than a high tech robot.

I rubbed my eyes once more. It was our former Principal Aileen and she stepped down to approach me.

"Hey Jim." Principal Aileen said.

"I thought you were zapped. I mean I'm glad you can make it to the race. What happened with your home planet?" I asked Principal Aileen and flattered by her silence.

"Well there's one thing." Principal Aileen said with a smirk.

"President Metal sent me back here, because of his affection for me." Principal Aileen added.

"That's not creepy at all. Thank you for coming! By the way, you weren't serious about expecting human extinction right?" I asked.

"No I wasn't serious. I don't know what the future holds for all of us including my species. Good luck on the race Jim." Principal Aileen said.

I found a new layer under those green slithered scales of her body. She was actually a decent person which is why I am now giving her title back as I meant it. She deserves that much from me after the gossiping that Mel and I did behind her back.

I seen Principal Aileen come back to her seat but this time remained sitting right next to President Metal holding his robotic hand. I didn't get too stoked for our president to be watching us unless they look similar to human or human themselves. President Metal is the only robot that doesn't have a human genetic makeup on them. This was ironic to hear coming from the year 3000.

I needed to get my mind back on track minutes before my first lap starts. I scan the audience to see if my parents or Myra ever showed up. Just by a glance down the right side of the mother ship I seen a light shine on my parents forehead and Myra sitting along with them. It just occurred to me I haven't got a chance to introduce them.

Mr Blank seen I was waving at them and whispered something to me.

"I introduced Myra to your parents. I'm sorry, I wanted to surprise you for being a excellent student and friend." Mr. Blank whispered to me while my head was back on the race at hand.

"Thanks, Mr. Blank!" I said with a huge smile.

"You're welcome and please call me Bobby." He replied.

Bobby Blank? That was a name like no other. I was just glad to see things are finally making sense for the betterment to fit in this virtual and high tech world.

I got into my stance as others finished sipping their waters and got into a line as well.

"Welcome ladies and gentleman, male and female aliens, male and female robots, male and females in general. We thank you all for joining us here tonight for our first annual A Race Through Time Competition. I am your host and a gym teacher as well, Mr. Blank. Soon, the ship is going to lift off and we will get started." Mr. Blank said so amused with his opening speech.

Everyone remained silent until we lifted off the hovering platform and went into outer space. Even us participants thought wow to the big surprise. The audience shouted and it was a loud shriek of noise. The good part is the anti-gravity in space made the competition a bit more challenging yet entertaining at the same time.

I ran and started moving my legs in a form of peddling being sent in the air by anti-gravity. It was actually pretty cool and I tried my hardest to land over my opponents in a hurry. Luckily, three of the robots ran beside each other got hit with a laser that caused them to move in slow motion. I was ahead of three opponents and so far there were five us in this first round. Each round had three laps and a person could sub someone in between those laps. The only rule we had was after they are subbed they would have to start all the way back from the start line. If they refuse to do this, they will forfeit their lap.

I looked over at Mel from the sideline and I can tell our telepathy is strong while he nodded back right at me.

I landed down after finding my control of the gravity pull. I was the first to finish on the first lap which gave me some competitive edge. I decided to take turns with Mel and subbed him in for the second lap. I heard my parents now screaming at the top of their lungs for me to stay in the whole round. I shook my head at the thought of playing it that long without a sip of water. I sipped water over a electric water fountain near the track circle.

I felt a rush run through me as Mel even was high up on the second lap. He didn't make first place, but he was the second one to finish the lap until the last lap of the first round.

Mel subbed me back in and I did a few stretches as we lined up once again. I ran fast as lightning, but this time the robot was lifted up by gravity as I hope he doesn't start pushing himself forward. I had my fingers crossed sprinting and dodging each laser beam until the last beam made me jet like the wind of a category five hurricane.

I finished in third place this lap, because I was neck and neck with the second place runner as he sped in front of me toward the finish line.

It was down to a few finalists including Mel and I. The loudness of the crowd grew higher and higher that all the robots covered their ears from destroying their high level sense of hearing. They even roared like a herd of lions and wildcats. I waved out to my parents and they responded giving me a salute. Mel waved back toward his folks as well, but they was too busy cheering loud and proudly.

We were back side by side with the other opponents. Mel decided to run while doing flips which I never knew he had that much of endurance in the past. I was smirking knowing both of us had that agility. The anti gravity began once again and this time lifted all of the participants which made this first lap a game of whoever lands on the finish line first. One of the participants got eliminated for kicking and shoving an opponent in the air for unsportsmanlike conduct. This left us up against one robot along with their female partner. Soon enough Mel finished second to the female opponent.

"Brief intermission, folks. Again, we will be having a brief intermission." Mr. Blank said to the crowd.

I went up to the stands where my parents and Myra sat. They were pleased to see me and congratulated how far Mel and I would be in the competition.

"See son, I told you technology has their pros more than the cons. Promise me you will always look on the positive side." My mom said before giving me a bear hug.

Myra smiled knowing my parents have no idea what her genetic background actually is. In contrast to what they believe she is inside and out, I still accept her as the lovely cyborg girlfriend I now adore.

"How was the race like? Did you feel powerful inside?" Myra asked.

"It was like running behind a bunch of laser pointers. Really, it felt like my dream. You know I keep a dream journal from time to time." I said wanting her to know everything.

"Wait, is that what I keep hearing you cite to yourself before school?" My mom asked.

"I thought you were preparing to present a project." My dad added.

"No, if that was the case I would have a bunch of assignments for one school year." I said laughing.

My dad laughed along with my smart comment. I went back down to my position knowing I'm up next for this second lap around the track course. As I walk down the stands, I notice Principal Aileen kissed the president metal face by leaning her head to the left of her.

"Yuck, but I am happy for that odd couple." I told myself.

I also seen Mrs. Mathews near the front section. I waved at her and she smiled waving back.

When we were out there side by side, I put on my game face which was my right eyebrow raised while keeping straight face. It gave me a competitive look that may psyche out my opponent.

Once the race started, I ran and ran as quick as I could sprinting through not worry about lasers in front of me. I almost fell out trying to dodge the last laser. Fortunately, I caught myself as I was a few inches ahead of my opponent considering robots are quick on their feet. The result of the second lap became a tied one. It had the crowd make a very grunting sound which meant they really was expecting more than a tie.

The judges took a minute to talk it over and they wanted us to keep going forward to the last lap. I asked Mel if he sure he didn't want to take this last lap for me. He insisted I get this win or lost for us both since I was lucky enough to tie up the last lap.

"You know what let's do this!" I exclaimed getting back out there.

This final lap, Mr. Blank held up a air horn and set it off on the count of three.

"1." Mr. Blank said.

"2." Mr. Blank continued after a moment of silence.

The robot legs started shaking and was sparking up a bit.

"And 3." Mr. Blank announced letting off the air horn that set off a loud boom.

I ran forward not looking back. The lasers came at me like rapid fire and I jumped over each of them like a ninja warrior. At last, I finished the race and there wasn't a single trace of the robot I was up against. I looked down the long stretch track course and seen the robot laid out at the starter line. I think his leg might've short circuited and now he's out like a rock.

I ran back over to it and tried to use one of the methods I learned from Mrs. Mathews. I tried to twist up a wire sticking out of its metal leg and gladly nothing sparked up considering my bare hands were exposed. The robot began to slowly move its finger and quickly jumped out of the way. It clicked in me that I may be good at fixing technology while also keeping in touch with my writing side. This honestly could've been the best day of my life.

Everyone paraded down their seats and the whole course swarm from humans, cyborg, robots and Principal Aileen. Principal Aileen was amused based on the fact she started to levitate smiling.

Mel gave me a handshake and we both complimented our skills out on the track. It was weird to think we would ever lose to a bunch of robots and five humans as their partners. If all the robots and humans were supposed to be paired up, Mel and I cheated this competition.

“Congratulations! Jim and Mel is our number one champions of A Race Through Time! Nice job son!” Mr. Blank exclaimed while I was in shock.

“Wow I get the son title now.” I said as I couldn’t believe this was all happening.

“Yes, you do. You guys raised a great kid.” Mr. Blank said to my parents.

“Thank you sir! You free to join us for a meal or just to hangout whenever.” My dad told Mr. Blank.

“Well, what do you guys say we eat later at my house? I might cook us some lamb chops with beans and rice.” Mr. Blank suggested.

My dad smiled thinking it over.

“We will be delighted.” My mom chimed.

“I was going to say yes.” My dad playfully told my mom.

“I know, but Mr. Blank is a busy man. You have to be direct and straight forward.”’ My mom insisted.

“I guess so.” I added jokingly.

Everyone shortly went back to their respected seats for the ceremony of receiving the metal and speeches from Mel, I and even the robot that was laid out name Ed.

“I sure hope you guys enjoyed this competition and it will warm our spirits if you all come next year as well.” Mr. Blank said over the microphone.

Minutes passed of crowd engagement as they shouted Jim and Mel repeatedly while clapping toward the end of their chant.

"Now we will have our winners start us off with a speech. Who want to go first?" Mr. Blank asked.

"Can we both go first, sir?" Mel asked while I nodded along.

"Yes, you may do as you wish. Be mindful of time in respect to the other runner ups beside you." Mr. Blank informed Mel and I.

"I want to say I am honor to win this especially with my best bud Mel by my side. I also want to take the time to let you all in one secret. That secret is that we should honor those not fortunate to see this techno plaza we live in today. There was a time where a disease called Covid-19 once plagued the earth in the years 2020 to 2023." I said.

The crowd gazed over at me and suddenly found laughter about every part of what I said.

"Umm, this is a serious matter. Don't y'all care about those people that created the inventions we love today?" Mel asked.

Only two people in the entire eighty thousand of the population nodded yes.

Mel handed me the microphone.

"I see we are a bit ungrateful, but I want you all to remember this. Time is precious and we can't take it back. At least talk to your love ones before turning your life into a digital rampage of future problems such as posture, shorten brain, and a loss of eyesight due to screens facing you all each and every day. Remember that and keep the hope alive." I said while Mel was in an awe at the podium.

I handed the microphone to my runner up smiling and began having two single tears run from each eye to the side of my cheeks. It may haven't touch their hearts yet, but it sure did mine and my heart is now yearning for others imagining those simpler times.

Before heading off the stage, I started hearing the middle of the robot's speech.

"And I wanted to make this clear for everyone. I love every being on this planet and I never ever want you all to be so dependent on my metal parts and advanced ways. Jim and Mel are certainly here to give you all praise at being human and certainly never try to be one of us. For one, I been operated to serve for humanity and not the other way around." The robot named Ed said as I applauded that last remark.

"That ladies and gentleman is what I'm all here for and that is unity. Such a beautiful speech given by each winner and one of our runner ups. Great job guys and thank you all for being apart of our A Race Through Time Competition!" Mr. Blank exclaimed.

Chapter 9-

THE YEAR 2020

After we ate and sat at Mr. Blank's house, we were at the table discussing where my mind was at giving that speech. I told them I wanted to accomplish reminding people who may have forgotten about previous years than just it being year three thousand. They insisted how beautiful and profound the speech was that it knock them out of their seats.

We went back home after such a long day. I rest like a baby later that night.

I dreamed of the year 2020 and even to my understanding of how it must've been like to be born during this time.

My dream starts off with me at a house which actually set foot on grass and soil. My parents only had cellular devices and I had a regular bed that didn't detect any sensory object or brought light to the room. I was amazed as if I was walking into a land of simplicity.

The year was officially 2020 as I slept. I further allow people to wave off to me in the distance. Even my legs felt stronger walking on the land and feeling sweet oxygen revive itself in and out of my lungs. I seen Myra there and she looked way different and completely human as well. I was walking with a stride step and went to talk to her. Unfortunately, she didn't know who I was and I tried to reintroduce myself. It worked like a charm and she was impressed that I wrote in a dream journal. Apparently, the kids in my dream barely talk to their parents due to smaller parts of technology like video games and laptops.

"Hey, you seen a Sky Raiser around?" I asked Myra.

"Sky, what now?" Myra asked me while I looked up at the sky like a lost puppy.

"Never mind, must've meant a plane or something." I said trying to stay relevant in my dream.

The weird feeling got to me seeing people walk around with masks that covered their mouth and noses. I felt like I was walking into another dimension. I was a few miles down the road where my house sat. I ran back as soon as possible seeing a stray dog out and about.

"Is everything alright son? Did something startle you?"

"Yes, there's a big dog outside." I said.

My parents faced each other and burst out laughing.

"That's the neighbor's dog and he's harmless. I go outside with you in case you are still scared."

"Oh yeah silly old me. Why would I ever be frightened by a creature like that?"

"By any chance, are there dinosaurs out right now? I mean, it is 2020." I added while my parents continued laughing.

"Sorry, but no son. They have been extinct many years and almost a million years since now." My dad said.

"You sure you are feeling okay? You not hallucinating, are you? Maybe you should wear a mask outside to protect you from quarantine." My mom said after asking me random questions.

“Yes, I forgot that was how life is now.” I said after reminiscing about the book The Plague That Started It All.

I haven’t got a chance to read far into that book. As I thought more about the book, I realize I’m living in a dangerous plague. I seen images of people falling out on their beds as sick as a dry cough.

I went to my room and for the first time ever I felt complete silence. When I say silence, I mean no static noises and the only motors I could hear were from the cars across the street.

“Hey Jim, me and your mother are going out for the night. Feel free to order something while we’re out.” My dad said while I couldn’t think of what to do next.

“Okay, I will call y’all if I get turned around with the order.” I said anxious to order in 2020.

The way we call it was zapping a few meals instead of placing an order.

I was surprised the internet was still here in 2020. I search up the process of placing an order. I felt like an alien not use to human interaction lost on earth. This is exactly what the dangers of time travel get you. I was like a student to every little thing and that might even be driving on an actual road. My parents been using the Sky Raiser since I was a infant and came out of a hospital as that was even a digital high tech emergency room. The late twenty nine hundreds was sure a time to be alive as my mind drifted.

The dream shows myself placing the order and accidentally sending it to the house with the enormous dog. I was tip toeing over to the house and almost tripped feeling jet leg from being in the sky all my life.

"Jim! You up! Teacher is getting worried!" Voices screamed out while the vision of the home shuttle risen.

The dream snapped out of focus and my eyes open in the middle of the home shuttle. My face was stuck and my jaw was wide open while every concerned face look down upon me. The teacher came into my vision in the corner of my eyes.

"Jim, you okay?" Mel asked me.

"Yes, I was just napping." I said.

"That was some nap. You seemed out of it lately."

"I don't know, it was like I was in my bed at night and dreamed a bit. Now, I woke up here." I explained.

"Son, you seemed like you were awake on the outside but it was clear as day you day dreamed. I don't know how you manage to put your space suit on correctly." The teacher said feeling like I haven't got enough sleep lately.

"Yeah, you're right. I must've trained too much that I haven't giving my eyes enough time to rest." I said to Mrs. Mathews.

"I understand that, but you should always get enough sleep at night. You understand?" Mrs. Mathew's asked while her eyes widen.

"Yes."

"Good, you mind sharing your dream with the class. What was it about?" Mrs. Mathews asked a bit off topic.

I sat up from laying out on the shuttle's platform.

"It took place in 2020. There was houses on land and the air felt clear as day. There was a sickness going around, but the crazy thing is there's a lot I don't know about 2020. This made me feel very odd inside." I said shaking my head.

"That's okay, Jim. It can be a lesson though you don't have to feel this way anymore since it was a dream. After all, nothing real come out of those anyway." Mrs. Mathews said brushing it off as just a figment of imagination.

I looked around at all the nodding expressions from each classmate with their space suits. I realize how lost everyone would be in the year three thousand. It may have been a figment of imagination or dream, but there is truth in the visions I saw since it related to that old book Mrs. Mathews suggested.

"I agree to a certain extent, Mrs. Mathews. That book brought a lot of truth in this certain dream of mine." I explained to the class and Mrs. Mathews.

"Oh fascinating. Yes class, there was a book passed down to me in my family and it was titled The Plague That Started It All. The author was an old ancestor of mine by the name of Jamel Rogers. He wrote it after the plague which brought a lot of memories to me being the latest generation to have it." Mrs. Mathews said while the eyes of the class burst wide amazed.

"Wow, I want to read it." Liz said raising her hand.

"I want to read it as well and is it on our digital shelf?" Mel asked.

"You all can read it as long as you zap it back to me with the pen zapper." Mrs. Mathews told the class.

"Also Mel, it's also available digitally. In that case, you can read it through the screen as well." Mrs. Mathews added toward Mel.

"Right, I have no problems taking turns." Mel said winking over at Liz in his space helmet.

I chuckled.

"Well, I'm glad Jim wasn't in any serious condition though just lack of sleep." Mrs. Mathews said to the entire class.

Liz looked up at the shuttle ceiling and raised her hand once again toward Mrs. Mathews.

"Yes, Liz"

"If there was no technology, how did he get his book published?" Liz asked.

"Who said there weren't any technology?" Mrs. Mathews asked.

Part of the class gave a confused look as some actually nodded as if they knew all along.

"See, they had technology just nothing like we see today. Who knows how life will be another thousand years from now or how humans will encounter each other and look?" Mrs Mathews asked while her questions repeated itself in my head.

"Oh, I understand. Thank you, Mrs. Mathews." Liz said excited to learn more.

Everyone in the class clapped their hands and one person in particular, Mel, suggested to use the entire shuttle to reinvent the year 2020.

Mrs. Mathews interrupted briefly to remind them that first they would have to learn more about the year before turning the home shuttle into it.

The home shuttle stayed silent as if a mime was performing themselves in a box.

"I'm not trying to rain on anyone parade, but class is officially over. I am glad that you all are interested in my ancestor's book. I'm excited for you all to discover great things inside it. Good luck now." Mrs. Mathews said as the ship dropped every person off to each address.

Mel hologram came back to the dead center of my bedroom in an instant and he climbed out of his blue pixelated self very slowly. I still couldn't get use to it.

"You sure that stuff is safe. I saw a bit of static from behind you crawling out of that contraption." I said not trusting this new update on the holographic watch.

"Hey man, it's easier than taking the Sky Raiser. I love this new upgrade." Mel said.

"That's possible. You just wanted to hang out bro or you had to ask me something?" I asked Mel.

"Yeah bro, can I possibly borrow that book of yours?"

"Oh yeah, sure thing. Remember to keep it in a safe place, bro." I reminded Mel.

I went to grabbed the book and suddenly it was gone. I almost torn my gadgets apart trying to find it. Then, I heard my mother being fascinated as she called me over to her room pod (room of gadgets).

Mel and I came to her room to find her with a cup of coffee reading in the middle of the book I was trying to find. We shrugged it off since she was clearly enjoying it and we went back to play some games on the televised ceiling. The graphics on the game was almost three dimensional. I was so into the jet racing game I didn't realize my mom was already finished with the book. I found it later outside of my sliding door.

"Hey bro, here's the book! Hope you enjoy bro!" I exclaimed to Mel.

"Thanks man! I'm ready to time travel into a whole new world and this book will do the trick." Mel said.

"Yes sir." I replied before he hopped into the Sky Raiser back home.

Strangely, I had a full appreciation of the year and can't wait for time to move even more forward. I thought maybe in the future or even thousand years ahead our legs will be made of steel. Only time can help me conclude this as a fact and not some random observation.

"Hey mom, how you like the book?" I asked.

"It was fascinating and I almost wish I can go back myself."

I thought about my mom's last remark and knew how I can make people remember the year 2020. I went to my bedroom to make a brainstorm in my dream journal. At this point, I was on the two hundred and eleventh page in my journal.

NAME: JIM / DATE: 7/01/3000 / DREAM JOURNAL

BRAINSTORM:

Simulation to 2020

Act out as a person in 2020

Give my parents food from 2020

And More…

I closed my dream journal and laid back playing some more video games. I wanted to pass my time down just to help my mind. I was never prouder than this moment here while I stared up at the televised ceiling. I got a dope dream journal full of ideas, a best friend, cyborg girlfriend, and won a first time competition called A Race Through Time.

When I thought about Myra, I realized I haven't spoke to her in a good while since the dinner at her dad's place. However, I do remember seeing her after I woke up to what felt like a two day coma.

I decided to call Myra's hologram and her pixelated presence appeared quick.

"How things going?" I asked.

"Well, I guess it's been good. I just never thought about what I should do this summer. It's really bumming me out." Holographic Myra said.

"Yes, I think we should just work on something together. It will do us a disservice not to show off our talents. I love to write and you love to talk in a group setting. We should work on a fire presentation for school next year reminding the others of 2020." I said with a huge smile and holographic Myra jumped excitedly.

"The year 2020. Well, guess we have to get in touch more often to complete that assignment." Myra said.

"That's a plus to it as well." I said hugging the hologram.

As I pulled back from the hug her arms stayed around my shoulders. I walked back and her actual self pulled away from the pixelated version.

"Aw, you too. Mel was just over and did the exact same thing. I have to get my upgrade soon." I said.

"Why haven't you got the upgrade?" Myra asked.

"I just don't think I trust it. No defense to you and Mel though." I said.

"Well defense taken. What are you afraid of happening? You think Mel and I will blow up dispersing pixelated versions of ourselves?" Myra asked me.

"Yes and no." I replied.

"Maybe." I soon added.

"Let's not argue, it's just a stupid update. They'll be more of those things in the near future." Myra said letting us agree to disagree.

I switched the topic and she was all ears along with a gazing smile. I told her about some of the things I brainstorm for my parents after hearing my mom be fascinated with the year two thousand and twenty.

"What was twenty twenty like for you?" Myra asked getting a bit personal.

"Didn't you heard in class?" I questioned.

"Yes and no." Myra mocked laughing along.

"Okay, I'll tell you. It was an experience of a lifetime, but toward the end of it I realize I didn't fit in with the time period. It was like a blessing to be there but a curse not to know anything coming into it. It was like trying a new sport and never getting the hang of it for me." I told Myra.

"Understandable. I was thinking you can cover both the benefits and cons of the year coming back. I believe this can tie up our lives now with the year twenty twenty." Myra replied.

I clapped slowly and got faster by the second and third clap. I can feel the genius of our group getting larger and larger to get an applause.

"You're really a great partner." I said.

"Thank you babe." Myra said.

Myra hopped back into her pixelated stance in the dead center of my bedroom. I waved goodbye toward her while she waved slowly placing her hand back toward her pixelated hand.

This technology is getting cooler by the second. I laid eyes on her pixelated hologram before the system shut off. It felt like the computer tools such as the gadgets in

Tony Stark's Iron Man Suit. As I thought about Iron Man, I knew even that was a classic movie during the era of the two thousands.

"Abracadabra." I said to myself with a huge grin.

I laid back on my light felt bed and had my bed set to river mode. The covers felt like waves splashed without a drop of water on the bed itself. The motioned bed seemed like a great investment my parents made to my bedroom. I turned on my televised ceiling and the news was on.

The screen displayed a news reporter in front of a laboratory announcing the first person to publicly be a participant of a Time Machine. I knew this was going to be basic suicide due to the dangers of time. I guess the guy must've been a rich guy wanted to go back to tell his ancestors.

"That's right folks, today we have a time machine and a person to try it out for the fifth time. Isn't this exciting news?!!" He asked.

"Well, we are going to live stream the whole thing for our people watching from their homes. Guess what Dale?" He continued asking his co-anchor.

"What's that, Miller?" Dale asked.

"It's set to take place in the year two-thousand and twenty. Will this be a big win for the Cleveland family or another failed experiment compared to old scientists years ago?" He asked smiling.

"Let me guess, anything can happen." Dale interrupted saying it sarcastically.

Then, he made air quotes as he repeated mouthing those words anything can happen.

“This really is a buzzkill. Time travel can only be in dreams and that is what I found out to be the case.” I said to the screen as I watched the program.

The news showed a gentleman named John Cleveland hopping into his time machine. Moments later, he scattered out as a small sized ant. The news anchorman tries to look for him as the timer on his watch ran out. Soon as he sees the ant, he motioned a stomp and I could tell by the sound of it, the ant or Johnson was under his right foot.

I slowly felt the intense stomp ringing through my ears and switched to another channel. I turned to a movie made in that year two thousand and twenty. After all, I couldn’t bring the year twenty twenty to me better than I come to that year through mediums such as movies, dreams, and books. I can feel times being simpler when I don’t try too hard as these scientists. The truth is time is never made to travel rather than save memories for others who weren’t born in it yet.

— THE END —

ABOUT THE AUTHOR~

Jamel Rogers is a twenty- four-year-old author. He currently resides in Midlothian, Virginia and has released three books such as Deceased: Secret Underworld,

The Shoreline on South Beach, and Picture This.

Mr. Rogers currently works as a full time English Teacher and Freelance Writer. He enjoys writing surprising plots and helping inspire today's youth.

In 2023, Jamel has entered a Television Writing contest, sponsored by Script Pipeline, with an adult animated pilot script titled: The Aggressors.

You can find more of his books at: https://www.amazon.com/stores/author/B07YBLJ51N

IF YOU ENJOYED IT OR WANTED TO SHARE YOUR THOUGHTS, FEEL FREE TO LEAVE A REVIEW UNDER CUSTOMER REVIEWS ON AMAZON!

Made in the USA
Columbia, SC
02 September 2024